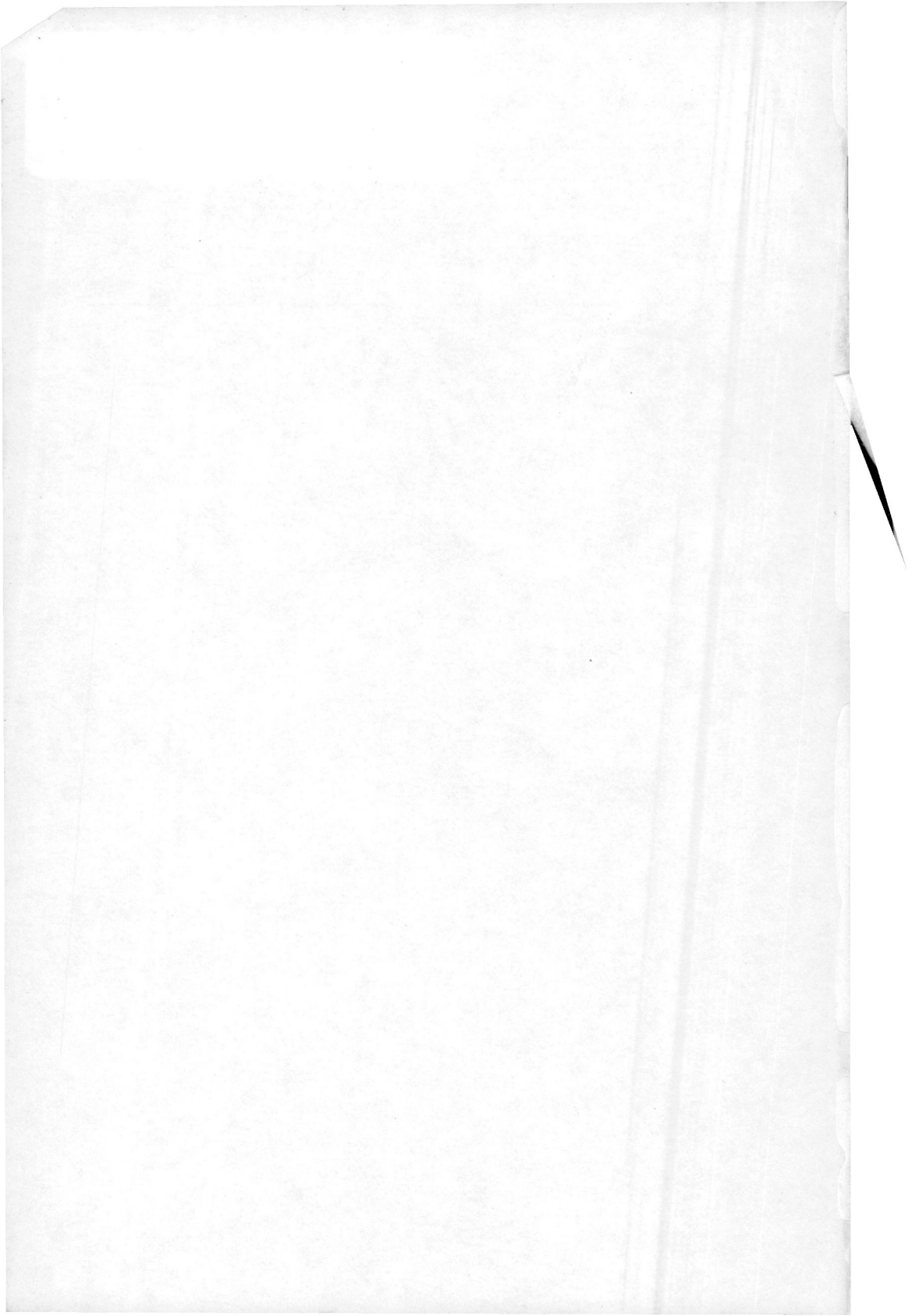

The Fate of Humanity:
A Demon's Perspective

The Fate of Humanity: A Demon's Perspective

From the Prophet
Zachariah Lehmann

Rev. date: 05/10/2016

To order additional copies of this book, contact:
Xlibris
1-888-795-4274
www.Xlibris.com
Orders@Xlibris.com
733410

This book is dedicated to my unborn daughter.
R.I.P. my sweetest girl.

"I'm a myth, I do not exist."- The Demon Belial.

Chapter 1

JOSHUA WAS IN the middle of the crowd. Maybe fifty to sixty—depends on who you ask. The warlock was on a fairly large block of wood made of logs. It was deep in the middle of the woods. The sun had just set, but it was still beautiful with the red and yellow behind the hills. This place was a myth in San Francisco. Nobody ever came to these woods except Legion. This space was ours.

No one—neither citizen nor the police—would enter unless they had to. Usually, it was the FBI and the cops trying to identify one of the many souls who had lost his or her life here. If you were new to town, you would eventually find out by word of mouth or, even worse, by ending up there after the sun went down, not knowing where you were. Bad shit usually happened then.

Josh's attention then went back to the stage, where a crying baby in the background would not stop wailing. Josh didn't know how he got there dressed in full cloak and hood. Way too much vodka. He was feeling it coming up, but he could still keep it down. His stomach was wrenching, he looked up and the show was starting.

At the altar stood the high priest speaking in Latin. Never heard one of these in Latin. Joshua had taken Latin 101 in college. He thought the high priest was saying, "God is dead," over and over. What a clown. He doesn't realize you can't have one without the other. It's the whole yin and yang thing.

Behind the altar were three crucifixes upside down and smeared with feces, mocking the Trinity. There was a black baby boy on the Alter contorting itself and wailing. One of the coven would go downtown and buy a baby from a meth addicted vagrant. Josh thought it was so sad. It was normally a cat, but mostly it was a goat. It made him uncomfortable but he could handle an animal sacrifice. "But a baby, this must be a special occasion," he though not knowing if he would be able to keep the vomit down.

The high priest stood and shouted in English, "Bring it up!" Two cloaked women with their breasts keeping their cloaks open came rushing up the stairs. They were carrying a snake-shaped small sword across their folded-out arms. The priest rushed at them, grabbed the sword, spit on them, and then turned and came back over to the baby. The baby was wailing. Now he was shouting in Latin. Man, he wished he was just at a regular black mass with the nice and distasteful orgies.

The priest grabbed the baby boy by the face and knocked the back of its head against the hard alter. He turned around, and then back toward the baby. He lunged and grabbed at the short sword on the Alter. Joshua turned away as this was happening. Was this actually happening? About two seconds later, the crowd roared and then chanted, "Feed! Feed! Feed!" Josh turned back towards the stage.

The priest was looking at the crowd with a psychotic look in his eye and blood running from his mouth, the crowd was still yelling in admiration. Everything kind of became a blur after that, now that the vodka had really kicked in.

Chapter 2

JOSH WOKE UP next to a girl from the ritual last night. He was such a sweet talker. If you were into BBW's. She woke and rolled over and looked at him with a big grin on her face. She asked Joshua if they could do breakfast, and Josh politely declined, citing a page within himself that he had to be at his parents' at 3 p.m. She asked if he would see her again, and he said with a smile, "I'll give you a shout sometime this week." He gave her a kiss, and she drove off with an angry look on her face. "Okay, another successful date." He laughed and went back into the house and grabbed a Strongbow cider, went out to the patio, and lit a joint. He started thinking about last night.

Sacrificing cats and dogs and disemboweling them was one thing, but an actual human baby was too much for him. Josh knew he was in with them now and it was almost impossible to leave. See, it's just not good to leave a coven. Those people have many harsh secrets and will kill anyone to keep those secrets safe. They always come as friends, but you have to look behind their calm and friendly demeanor.

They were mostly people of power and prestige, or who had been invited in by one of them. And then for some, it didn't matter about their background. They were just hard-core into evil. They were the scary ones. They were the ones who provided the human sacrifices at the Sabbats. They were the ones who orchestrated the Sabbats. It was kind of like watching a play in the way the plot was always changing.

But it was always one of three: human sacrifice, animal sacrifice, or orgy, which was far and away Joshua's favorite. He never got into the sacrifices and killing. He found it very unnecessary, and it made him quite uncomfortable, but he would never mention that to anyone in the coven. He had tried to leave in the past, to no avail. He knew if he left, he could be taken out at any time. Brakes clipped, gas leak in the house, hit and run—maybe even a straight fucking bullet to the head. These situations all awaited him. And the lifestyle was actually a part of him now. He had conjured up some what he thought to be minor demons, and he was even granted a familiar for a week that came in the form of a crow that spoke to him and told him some very interesting things.

He was twenty seven, a drunk, still in school part time, and a bartender at a club on San Francisco's main strip. It was often frequented by gay clientele. Josh never had an urge to chug cock, and they all respected that. Except that they did occasionally grab his ass, which he despised but endured for good tips. This led him to some heavy drinking nights and lots of after-hour parties. A lot of raves with those fucking glow sticks and all fucked up on E, lot of gay guys hitting on him who he would have nothing to do with, and the occasional beautiful mod chick who, when drunk, loved to take it in the ass.

Every Friday and Saturday he did his after hour drinking at the Matador. It had a straight clientele for the most part. It was like a big underground warehouse with a huge stage in the front, then rows of benches and tables, and then a huge dance floor that was always hopping. You would get your mickey from the little Mexican girl in the corner for twenty dollars and then get the mix from the waitress.

They had such an awesome setup: some of the best rock bands that he ever heard and every once in a while, a cool Goth or industrial band. Yeah, people would get stupid sometimes. That happened when people drank straight from eight at night till five thirty in the morning. But there was always this bouncer, Alfy, who stood up for the good guys. Joshua even helped sometimes for fun. He was a big boy. Alfy and Josh were pretty close.

He would go to the club and instead of dancing with the beautiful girls, he was with Alfy getting hammered and talking for hours on end. Being raised a Catholic, Joshua had a definite interest in the dark side. Alfy knew much about the subject. Some of the regulars were Devil worshippers and there was also a lot into voodoo. Alfy would talk of rights and rituals, sacrifices and conjuring demons, even though he had never delved himself.

It was one Saturday night and Alfy and Joshua were talking. He had been at the club for a while and had pretty much drunk a twenty sixer

ZACHARIAH LEHMANN

to himself, plus the drinks he got in him after work at the club when he stumbled over to the matador at about five am. Alfy was talking to a beautiful, black-haired girl with bright green eyes and the nicest ass in the room. She was wearing skintight lulu lemon black pants with no underwear. Alfy stood up and looked at him and said, "Do you know what she needs?" This is Jade."

He whispered in her ear and they both chuckled. She spun around on a dot, and said "Hey, come dance with me," with the most cunning smile. Who could resist? So he was swinging her around and doing the jig himself. He was not the best dancer.

Then she pulled in close to his ear and panting said, "I like you." "I want you to know what I'm all about." Pick me up at Twenty Second and Forty Third tomorrow at eight thirty."

Joshua happily nodded his head. Then she put on an innocent little face, blew a kiss, got her girlfriend, and ran out of the club. Josh was very enticed. He hadn't had a girl that he was that attracted to in a while. He left the place pretty quick too. As he left he could see the sun just about to pop its head over the horizon. It was still dark out, but the sky had a reddish tint to it.

Chapter 3

HE SLEPT TILL about 5 p.m. the next day and then got up and had a nice steak and spinach salad. He started drinking again, Strongbow cans, until he went out. He was at the corner five minutes ahead of time with a can in his lap. He was driving his black cherry '77 Firebird, fully restored. It was the one with the 454 and the T bar roof. It had the firebird in white on the hood and had big black slicks and wicked rims.

Jade then walked up from behind the car. She was beautiful, wearing a skintight, one-piece, short, short dress that was cut just above the bottom of her ass cheeks. He got an immediate erection. "So what's up, honey?" Josh said, with his Ray Ban's on and a big smile on his face.

"I love your car," she said with a big smile, her blue eyes and black hair shining. "Jump in," Josh said. She slid into the car laughing and lighting a smoke. "So what do you have in store for me tonight?" Josh asked curiously. She looked over and smiled, "This is the night I'm going to show you what I'm all about." "Don't be scared," she said chuckling, it's going to be a great ride, and they took of down the road.

They had been driving for an hour up some country road. The sun was down now and you could see the lights from the city. Josh didn't think she knew where she was going. "This isn't my regular hang out." "I'm usually deep in the forest watching the high priest kill something, while I'm up to the real thing," she said with an evil grin.

"This is just to see if you can handle the real thing" Jade said. "I've heard that you've been to a few rituals, I also know you want to leave your coven and that you're scared of the repercussions." "There's different covens that practice down at the reservation park." "I guarantee if you hang out with me, no one will be after you." "This is all about the dark one." "About the fall of angels and the creation of the underworld, and who really runs the show up here or down here, whatever way you look at it," Jade said.

"Turn left," she said. It was now down a narrow dirt road that lead right up to this farmhouse. They pulled up and a beautiful women came out of the house. Jade flew out of the car and gave her a big hug. They started speaking in Spanish, then the woman had a dirty look on her face. She shrugged and took off back into the house. Jade walked back to the car and jumped back in. "We got to go somewhere else she said, they don't take to kindly to strangers tonight," she said.

"What the fuck," Josh thought. She leaned over and started rubbing his hard on over his pants. "Don't worry," Jade said, "we're going to have fun either way tonight." At that moment Joshua would have done anything she said. "Just pull out and go right," she said, as they sped off into the night. At about ten thirty that night they arrived at a parking lot of the conservation area he knew all to well.

"This is where I wanted to take you in the first place, and I found out it was a go," she said." "The summer solstice is coming up in a few days." "There's a really big build up to it." "So what does that mean," Josh asked. "That means one of the biggest parties of the year".

"Are you religious." "I am like a lot of people," Josh replied, "I was when I was a kid, but I fell pretty quickly out of it when I got older." They got out and started walking to the fire glow they saw deep in the brush. It was the same woods Josh went to with his other coven. She turned to him and with her smile said, "don't worry, I got you covered baby," as she tugged and they started a light jog towards the fire.

They got to the fire and there was about one hundred people there singing and chanting to the death metal band that was on the make shift stage. The band started playing "Sabbath, Bloody Sabbath," by Black Sabbath. They were actually pretty good, but the guitarist was no Tony Iomi. They made it to the center and where they started jumping and dancing with everyone else.

There were people climbing up on the stage and spitting on an inverted cross behind the band. There was a large man dressed in a cloak behind an alter on the stage that seemed to be praying very hard. Then he pulled up a cat by the scruff of the back of its neck and slit it's throat with a sharp dagger. He held the cat above his head and let the blood drip in his mouth. Then the song stopped and the band started playing a really heavy guitar tune solo.

Just then the crowd started stripping down and they started to perform sex acts. Jade started rubbing her ass in her tight dress against Josh's erection in his jeans. She was smiling at him and then they were face to face." "Here, take this," she said and gave him a pill. Josh took it down with another sip of his Strongbow without hesitation. He had picked up more at the corner store on the way there. For some reason he wasn't afraid of her at all, which had got him into trouble with other girls in the past.

Then suddenly Jade dropped to her knees and took Josh's penis out of his pants and started stoking it hard, but he was already hard. As she started performing felachio, Joshua looked over beside the stage and back towards the brush. He could make out a figure, it was bigger than him and the silhouette had horns and what seemed to be a tail and wings.

Three witches were running over to the figure and stared performing crude sex acts. Then the demon seemed to look over at him directed in his line of vision. The beast had big piercing red eyes and Joshua could feel his presence from a distance. He could hear the demon in his head say "let go, feel that power within you that wants you to let go," and then he heard a sinister laugh. It scared the shit out of him.

But he had to get back to the task at hand. This is when Joshua got down on his knees himself, pushed her skirt up over her ass and took her hard from behind. She began to moan deeply. She turned her head around and said, "See, I knew you could get into this." That's as much as Josh remembered.

ZACHARIAH LEHMANN

Chapter 4

H E WOKE UP on the top sheets in his bed Jade curled up right next to him. "How did I get here," he was talking to himself. Jade was sleeping next to him and wasn't startled by him. He ran to window and checked the driveway. The car was there but it was parked diagonally across the lawn. He walked over to the closet and pulled out a nice down comforter. He went and put it on Jade. She grabbed the edge of the blanket and hid her face. He let her sleep. Josh got out of bed and realized there was no way he could keep any food down that morning.

He looked at the back of the fridge and there were four Strongbow cans. "Wow nice," he thought. He got one out and cracked it, then went back to the bedroom to close the door. From then he was on the couch for the next couple hours. He got out the bong and took it nice hit right into his lungs. Best weed he ever had, it was AK-47, very expensive and hard to find. But it had a hint of a hallucinogen which gave it a nice kick. He would sometimes hear voices telling him to do strange things and he often saw the shadow a small boy in his apartment or the woods where he took his walks. But it could have been the schizophrenia kicking in. He watched TV for about two hours and was done the all the ciders. He had been trying to drink slow but now it was definitely time to hit the liquor store.

He peaked in the door and she was still out cold, with the comforter over her head. He got the keys on from the kitchen and took off. He was back within twelve minutes with a twelve pact. Josh walked up to the porch and open the door. "Hey hunny, where you been," Jade asked at him from his couch. She got up on the couch cushion and lifted her night shirt just over her nipples and said, "you want some more of this, baby." He chuckled looked at her and said, "very much," "but I just need my supper first pointing to the 12 pack."

"Are you hungry," Josh yelled at her from the kitchen. "No," she said, "ill grab my sushi down on the strip if you don't mind." "Not at all my dear, would you care for a beverage." "I only have the Strongbow I just got from the store, we drank almost everything else last night." "Son of a bitch, well Strongbow isn't so bad." He went over and sat next to her on the couch and handed her a can. "So what did you think about last night, do you think it's something you'd like to explore further," she said grinning.

"Absolutely, everything was great from what I remember before my blackout." "What was that pill you gave me," he said laughing but concerned at the same time. "Oh shit, you blacked out," Jade said concerned. "It was a ruffie," she said giggling. "It effects people differently, sometimes good, sometimes a blackout." "As long as you remember the sex, you were really hot last night." "No more of those, ok." "OK," Jade replied as if she thought there was nothing wrong with it.

"I don't know, there's just something about doing it with other people around appeals to me." "It felt good to let me unleash," he said grabbing her hip and body and placing it on top of his. They had a passionate kiss and Joshua threw his head back. "I think you're going to tell me something really fucked up right now," he said. "No, but I will once I get another cider," she said. "Grab me one too." Josh was looking at the moon and it was one of those black red moons that was so big he thought it would take over the planet. He put the next joint in his mouth and lit up.

It was about four o'clock and he had to work at the bar at seven. She came back and cracked a cider and gave it to him. "So witchcraft goes a lot deeper than what happened last night," she said. "Sex is fun and is a big part of it, but I'm going to have to teach you some rites and spells and how to conjure up some friends with some great power." "He looked at her feeling drunk and stoned and asked, "what kind of friends." "Major demons, minor demons, ghosts, familiars, entities like that." "Sounds like fun," he said, not thinking of the implications.

Even though he was Catholic growing up, he had never fell contact with God and he didn't believe God had helped him in his life. "It will completely change your life," she started. "Josh, I don't just pick up

ZACHARIAH LEHMANN

anyone, I can see things and I see something inside of you that seems to be like a magnet for those on the other side." "Have you picked up on anything supernatural in the past."

"I've never told anyone this but when I go to funerals and cemeteries, I hear the spirits from the ground talking to me in my mind," Josh said looking perplexed. "What do they say," she asked. "Help me, please do this for me some say, then there's the evil ones that tell me to hurt or kill, and they tell me I'm going to hell." "Wow, crazy," she said. "Does that happen anywhere else but cemetaries." "No where else, I'm no schizo hun," he said, and they both laughed. "Little did she know," Joshua thought.

Chapter 5

OSH STARTED TO tell her a story from his past. "When I was young I was an Alter boy." "The priest was a huge Irishman named James Masterson." "After service he would always come to me and we would talk about the bible and the book of Revelation." "Nice thing to talk to a seven year old boy about, eh," he said with a grin and a lost look in his eyes. "One day Masterson asked me to come in for a morning service during the week." "I didn't know why because the weekday services were pretty low key and not too many attended." "While giving the sacrament of communion at the mass, I looked in his eyes and stuck my tongue out to receive the blessing."

"His pupils had turned black and Masterson had the most evil grin on his face." "I was puzzled and really scared." "After the service when everyone was gone, he told me to come to the basement with him and that he would perform a special blessing on me that would purify my soul." "What a line eh," Josh said laughing.

"I knew there was something terribly wrong but what could I do, all my life to that point I was taught to listen and respect the Priest." "Masterson walked over and grabbed my hand and we went down into the church basement." "When we got down there, Masterson grabbed a bottle of Jaimson's off his work bench." "I remember the musty smell down there."

"He led me into a storage room with the Christmas decorations, old posters and flyers, and a damaged pew." "He began to sing an Irish tune to himself and dance around a bit." "He must have been drinking before the service because he was totally smashed." "Then he turn to me and he had a thin rope in his hand." "He said to me, Joshua, no matter how much you let the good Lord into your life and accept his son as your savior you will always, always be a sinner."

"You will always experience pain and doubt about whether all the prophet's stories are true." "Nothing is tangible and you will always be going on blind faith." "The only think that is tangible is the pain you feel." "I'm going to make you experience extreme pain to cleanse you," he said slurring and wearily," "You need cleansing." "Put your hands behind your back Masterson told me." "I didn't know what to do, I did what he said, but I was so scared I pissed myself." He tied my hands in a tight not, and then he began to raped me," Josh said in a low voice and with a blank stare.

"Afterwards, he came over to me and dropped to his knees." "He covered his face with his hands and wept." "You little shit, why did you seduce me, why did you seduce me he repeated over and over." "By that time I had fallen over in pain and exhaustion." He then untied me and told me to get up but I couldn't stand." "He lifted me up and carried me up the stairs while he was still weeping." "He threw me out the back door of the church into the garden and said, when you can walk, get the fuck away from here."

"I don't care if you go home or not, but don't tell anyone about this or I will gut you and put you where no one will find you." "He turned and took a huge swig of his Jaimison's, and slammed the door of the church behind him."

"I laid on the lawn in shock, I could have died from the shock that day." "I felt my underwear filling up with blood from my anus." "I laid there for about 2 hours I guess, couldn't really tell you how long, thinking I was dying."

"I was listening to the birds singing and the sun shone down on me." "The warmth was so nice on my face." "I finally gained the courage to try and stand." "After falling over a few times, I staggered a bit but was able to stand." "I stood for a couple of minutes then began to limp and stagger the four blocks towards home." "I got to my front door and got inside."

"My parents weren't home and I began climbing the stairs, very carefully and slowly, step by step." "It was so painful, I started crying again and I flopped down on the bed and proceeded to talk my clothes off." "I very painfully stood up again and made my way to my bathroom." "I turned the water on in the bathtub and turned the shower on and got in sat down in the tub as the water hit my body, I hung my head and watched the blood bleed from my ass down the drain." "I was still in shock."

"After the shower I went down to the washer and washed my clothes." "And by the time my mother was home I was lying down in my bed and shivering in my PJ's." "Hi sweetie, she yelled from downstairs, how was school." "Fine, I just said in a low voice." "Ok good, I'm just going to watch my soap, I'll make dinner real soon." "After about a half hour I got enough courage to go down the stairs." "She was sitting on the couch and I waddled over and hung my head."

"She looked very concerned and asked me what was wrong." "I said, while crying, that Father Masterson asked me to come in this morning to help with the morning service." "I told her he hurt me, he hurt me real bad, and that I was bleeding out my bum." "She hung her head and started to weep and wail."

"She got up and I'll never forget this." "She walk over to me and slapped me with her back hand and then grabbed me by the chin and said, you can never tell anyone about this, ever, and that if she ever found out that I told, there would be consequences." "Then she hugged me and helped me upstairs to my bed." "She brought my dinner up to me that night." "I have no idea what she told my father but that following Sunday we went to the Church across town." "I stopped going to church when I was old enough, around fifteen."

"That's the most horrible story I have ever heard Josh," Jade said crying and hugging him." "There are some really fucked up people in this life, and someone of them we know from the coven, but you have to look past that." "That piece of shit will get his." "I know, Joshua said and they huddled and cried on the floor for a bit." "Nothing ever happened to me like that, I was just invisible to my family and spent as much time away from home as possible."

"They didn't even care when I started in with the wrong people and got so bad into the meth." "They threw me out when I was seventeen." "I would stay with any dealer that would feed my habit, and sold my body for them." "I wasn't even mad when they kicked me out," Jade continued, "I Just didn't want to leave my baby brother there with them, but I didn't have a choice." "I'd go and meet him after school and walk him part way home." "He always loved me and never looked down on me, no matter how high I was."

ZACHARIAH LEHMANN

"Then one day I was too dope sick to leave my bed and didn't meet him." "I went to school the next day, and he didn't come out of school." "I went into the office and told them who I was and asked where my brother was." "The secretary got on the phone and called the Principal." "She sent me into his office." "The principal had a stern but concerned look on his face."

"I know the situation that you and your parents are in," he said. "I also know how much you loved your brother." "That's why I'm talking to you about this." "Jade, John's gone," he said. "I didn't understand what he was telling me at first." "He said that John was waited for me for a while, then he took off home." "He said a drunk driver had jumped the curb and hit him while he was walking down the side walk." "I'm so sorry," the principal said sincerely." "I just said thank you and quickly made it down the hall towards the doors".

"As soon as I got outside I walked over to the grass, I bent over and puked, fell to my knees and started screaming at the top of my lungs incoherently and then I just fell over and started weeping for about five minutes." "I was just thinking the only day I don't go to meet him, he's killed."

"I wished so much that I had have been with him and got hit too, because I didn't want to live either." "I looked over and saw the principal come out of the building and other people staring standing watching me." "I got up and started running down the road." "John wasn't just a part of me, he was the only family I had left and I truly loved him more than anything else on earth."

"When I got home I just went in and ran for the heroin." "I took as much as I had to try and overdose, mainlining it." "I didn't think I could live with the guilt and shame of not showing up for him that day." "I woke up in the hospital the next day and spent two weeks in there recovering." "My depression took over for a long time after that," Jade said sadly. They both sat in silence for a few minutes holding each other and taking in the pain from the memories.

"I Think we should start some rituals and rites in the next couple of days, these entities can give you what you need in life, what your craving," Jade finally said after the pause. "But at what cost," Josh thought to himself. "Yeah sounds good," he said to her, she was everything he ever wanted in a girl and could not say no to her. "You know what the funny thing is," he said, "this is probably the most normal relationship I've been in about 14 months." They both laughed. Just then she looked over and smiled at him while undoing his zipper. "Ooh, alright," he said. They had passionate but violent sex before he went to work.

ZACHARIAH LEHMANN

Chapter 6

IT HAD BEEN two weeks and Jade had pretty much moved in, but Josh didn't mind at all. They had been doing séances and performing spells and trying to conjure up what they could using the Book of Black Magic and of Pacts. Nothing huge had happened yet. Joshua had tried to control the weather and conjured up a pretty wicked thunderstorm. They had tried to conjure demons but except for a few vicious voices and whirling wind, they were unsuccessful. It was a cold and dreary night. The wind and the rain was so bad it was coming in sideways. They were trying to conjure the spirit of Alastair Crowley.

They began performing a spell that they thought could bring Alastair to them. After they had repeated the spell three times a dark form with the outline of a human form appeared in front of them. It looked like a human black hole. The form was black, but shaped as a human but with no eyes or any distinct features. Josh couldn't believe it, he just stood in awe. Jade stood up and asked Crowley "how can could help us on their journey into the abyss." Crowley was a magician and an occultist from the turn of the 20th century who was adept at dealing with spirits, including powerful demons.

"First of all, you call me Beast," Crowley snarled. "Joshua thought this was for his ego more than anything, but he later found out that this is what his mother had called him. "Go to the clearing in the woods where you were before for the black mass and then continue north, the direction of Satan where he controls." "There you will find a place where two foothills intersect."

"When you look at the foothill to the right, you will see a small cave." "That's where you will meet the demon." "Don't worry, I will send a friend to guide you." "You will know when you see him." "I usually like to entice some sexual degradation for those about to sell their souls for my pleasure, but Josh, I know what happened to you with the priest." "I will not subject you to that." "His name is Astaroth and what you seek will become clear when you speak with him."

"You can only summon him between ten and eleven pm on Wednesday." "Tomorrow is Wednesday." "He is a good friend who is to be treated with the utmost respect." "He has been following your path." Alastair looked at them and smiled, "Im giving you a great opportunity," he said speaking to Joshua. "There will be another there, an entity of great importance." "He has extreme power, but I won't say anything else, you will see for yourselves."

"He was the second demon created after the fall, after Lucifer." "He's evil that you cannot comprehend." "He will come as the most beautiful image you have ever seen." "He won't do you harm but heed my warning, fear him, he is of absolute evil." Crowley started walking away from them and then disappeared into the dreary night.

"Holy fuck," Jade said, "can you believe this." "See I told you were powerful", she said to Josh. Josh just stood with a blank look on his face. "I'm a little scared," Josh said. "There's is nothing to fear, that the demon is expecting us." "He will offer something powerful but will expect something in return." "Are you ready to sell your soul Josh, for which you most covet."

"Josh, I've been into black magic for three years and something like this has rarely happens." "I'm so very excited for tomorrow, we should go out and celebrate." Josh had to work that night, but he called in sick. He knew this was the beginning of a huge change in his life, something sinister but enlightening. And he had Jade, the most important of all things.

ZACHARIAH LEHMANN

Chapter 7

THEY WOKE ABOUT one pm the next day. He and Jade spent part of the day studying about Astaroth. He was a male demon who evolved from the ancient Phoenician mother goddess of fertility. Astarte or Ashtoreth. Astaroth is also the FALLEN ANGEL and 29th of 72 SPIRITS OF SOLOMON. He was a high ranking ANGEL, either one of the seraphim or a prince of thrones, prior to his fall. Astaroth is a grand duke and treasurer of Hell and commands 40 legions of demons. Astaroth teaches all sciences and is keeper of the secrets of the past, present and future. He will give true answers to questions about the past, present and future. He encourages slothfulness and laziness.

The demon is said to instigate cases of demonic possession, most notably that of Loudun nuns in France in the 16th century. The nuns accused a priest, Father Urbain Grandier, of causing there possession. At Grandier's trial, a handwritten confession of his was produced detailing his pact with the Devil, witnessed by Astaroth and other demons. Astaroth loves to talk about the creation and the fall, and the faults of angels. He believes he was punished unjustly by God, and that someday he will be restored to his rightful place in heaven.

They found a spell that they thought would conjure the demon and declared themselves ready. Josh and Jade had a late dinner and shared a bottle of wine and toasted to having a great experience that night.

Over dinner, Jade started speaking about one of her conjuring's. "I was alone in the woods, where we're going to tonight." "There must be something about the area there has to be a vortex there between us and another place, a very bad place." "I was trying a few spells to conjure the demon Azazel." "I had made a pentagram in the clearing with a dagger."

"I slit my both wrists vertically, and it was bleeding pretty bad." "I walked around the pentagram dripping blood and then in the center." "That was part of my problems that night, you should never enter the circle." "I said the final part of the spell and then bandaged my wrists up." "I waited for about two minutes then saw a red glow in the brush and I moved towards it."

"I got closer and closer, and then I saw a red figure emerge ahead of me." "Azezel was in front of me." "He had this horrible pig face, huge horns and pointed ears." "The upper torso was a man's, but from the waist down he was a beast." "A goat had been following him and then sat down next to him."

"You summoned me and now I am here," he said with a smile and a squeal. "He started talking to me about the apocalypse." "He said that the end would happen in the next five years and that there would be many signs." "He said there would be a great war that would be waged between the angels of heaven lead by the Trinity and Arch Michael, against the demons of the underworld, led by the Dark One and his army, over the rites to mankind."

"He said that a quarter of the world's population where now atheist and that these people are at the heart of the dark one." "The greatest soldiers because they have denied God in their lives." "During great battle, Michael will betray his God and will fight for legion." "These soldiers, along with Michael's betrayal, is what tilted the tide for Legion."

"Praying on my vanity," Jade continued, "Azazel granted me eternal beauty and guaranteed I would have a place with the master when the end comes." "You will not burn, you will a powerful presence in Hell." Azazel told me. "Now for your part." "He walked over to her and disrobed me." "He began sucking on my breasts and then took me down to the ground and proceeded to rape me." "I'll never forget the rotting smell of him." "His penis was like a slithering snake inside of me."

"He grunted like a pig and drooled all over me." "He finished off with a great orgasmic squeal and left me lying on the ground, beaten and breathless." "My soul was his as soon as he entered me." "He stood up looked down on me and said, "do the will of the master and all will be well." " then he began walking with the goat back into the forest.

ZACHARIAH LEHMANN

"Wow, Shit, when did this happen," Josh asked. "About a year ago," Jade said. They sat and talked about more of their experiences.

It was eight O'clock and it was time they headed out. They got into the car and headed toward the conservation area." "I have no idea what to expect," Joshua said. "Just keep an opened mind and be respectful to the demon and it will be fine," Jade replied. "I do want to be wealthy, and have power and happiness, and you," Josh said to Jade. "My soul is a lot to give up for earthly pleasures," Josh said concerned. "He will probably will just ask for a sacrifice and for you to worship him," she said. "I don't know what's going to happen, we'll soon find out, but I'll be there for you," she said.

The sun was continuing to go down behind the hills. As they were driving the Stone Roses came on the radio. [I don't have to sell my soul, he's already in me, I don't have to sell my soul he's already in me, I want to be adored, I want to be adored, you adore me, you adore me.] They looked at each other with eyes wide open. When Josh returned his gaze to the road all the sudden there was a huge deer standing on the edge of the road as they wizzed by. He didn't even have time to react but they didn't hit it. He was just standing there waiting for them to pass by. But it was so close, he didn't know how he didn't hit it. If he had, all three of them would be dead. "Did you fucking see that," Josh asked. "See what," Jade said. "Never mind," he said gasping.

Chapter 8

THEY REACHED THE conservation area around nine o'clock. The sun was just setting on the horizon and there was a great display of reds and yellows. The moon was already in the sky. It was a new moon. Josh and Jade had a compass, flashlights and a gas lantern. They looked at each other and Josh still looked scared. "You cannot show fear or the demon will eat you alive, and remember they tell lies," Jade said. "This is all about you Joshua, I've already had my experience."

"I'm going to be with you in the cave but you will do all the talking and make all the decisions." "We're not dealing with just any demon, this is a grand duke of hell." "He has immence power." "You must realize you are a mortal dealing with a Diety." "Don't be frightened, just be aware of what you're dealing with." She continued. He nodded and pointed the compass and they started heading north.

It was difficult to get through the bush with branches scratching at their arms and then they found a path. Ahead about 25 yards they saw a huge beast. It seemed to have the body of a panther that was about eight feet long, but had the head of a dog with huge piercing red eyes. It was standing in the middle of the path just staring at them. All the sudden the black dog turned its head and started walking down the path slowly so they could keep up. "This must be the friend Crowley had promised," Jade said. "Let's follow, but don't get to close," she said.

The sun was completely down now and they were using their flashlights. Every time they stopped they would hear rustling in the brush. Joshua caught the dark figure moving a couple of times and then it would just disappear. It was definitely following them. They decided it must be Crowley watching them, he must be getting off on this.

Joshua checked his cell phone, it was nine thirty and nothing yet. They travelled for about another fifteen minutes and then the black dog turned and looked at them again. They caught up with him and then followed him to the left through the brush. Then they came upon the clearing where the foothills intersected and they saw the cave to the right.

Now Crowley's dark figure was visible as he stepped out of the woods. The black dog ran up to him and sat in front of him at attention. He pet his head and said "go home my pet," and the black dog took off into the brush. "Please enter," he said. Jade and Joshua entered the cave.

Josh lit the gas lantern and the small cave was illuminated. Then they saw Crowley's figure at the entrance of the cave. He laughed loudly and then said, "its so nice that you have made it." "Are you ready to meet your new god and pledge allegiance to him." "I am," Josh said hesitantly as he began to outline the inverted pentagram with his heel in the dirt on the cave floor. It was about now about ten fifteen, "What are we supposed to do now," Josh asked. "Just wait." Jade began to recite the spell to conjure Astaroth.

"Astaroth, Ador, Cameso, Valuerituf, Mareso, Lodir, Cadomir, Aluiel, Calniso, Tely, Plorium, Viordy, Cureviorbas, Cameron, Vesturiel, Vulnavij, Benez meus Calmiron, Noard, Nisa Chenibranbo Calevodium, Brazo Tabrasol, Venite, Venite, Astaroth. Shemhamforash!"

Jade said it with such passion going down on her knees and lifting her clenched fist upwards. She looked drained and curled up in a fetal position. About five minutes passed and then they saw a glowing orb about the size of a basketball enter the cave floating above the pentagram. It flew by them about ten feet deeper into the cave and slowly began to grow in size. It grew to be about seven feet tall and wide. It looked like a big black whirlpool spinning quickly counter clockwise. They began to see something step out of the portal. Astaroth suddenly appeared.

He appeared as an ugly presence, riding a small scaly green dragon and holding a viper in his hand. He was wearing a crown and had huge black dead eyes. The smell of him was so bad that it made Josh and Jade cringe. "Hello Jade, nice to see you again," the demon said, "thank you for coming." "Azazel sends his regards," Astaroth said to Jade then he grunted like at pig at her and giggled. Jade smiled and nodded. "Joshua, I am here for you," Astaroth continued. "What questions do you have for me?"

Josh stood stunned, there was so much going through his head. "We met at a Sabbat," Jade explained to Josh, "but it was very brief." "I'm sorry I didn't tell you before but it was just a brief meeting." "I didn't think he'd remember." "Of course I remember, I'm a demon," Astaroth said. "It's not like I forget anyone, no matter how brief the meeting." Astaroth smiled and said to Josh, "just let your head slow down so we can talk." The viper was staring right at Joshua, tongue out and lunging at him. Joshua rubbed his head and starting getting his thoughts together. He started thinking about his mother and father again.

Chapter 9

AFTER THE INCIDENT with the priest, his father had left them and Josh grew up with his mother in Tacoma, Wasahington. She had gotten into heroin heavily after the incident. She made her money as a prostitute. Joshua would go days without seeing her, but he always had food, beer and weed. When he did see her, it was if she was in a catatonic state, rail lines all up and down her arms and legs. She would sometimes come into his room after doing the drugs, when she was sober and held him and told him over and over that everything would be ok. This made Joshua uncomfortable. He would try to talk to her, to reason with her about the drugs, but it was as if she was already dead.

When he was twelve years old, during one of her tricks, a john named Keith had slit her throat and killed her. He and the priest were the only ones at her funeral and at the graveyard after. After the funeral, he was sent to live with foster parents because his father had never loved or even liked him since the Masterson incident. His father called him the son of the whore. Josh new that his father hated him because of what had happened with the priest. Before the incident they had been a happy, God fearing family.

On Josh's eighteenth birthday, his father arranged a meeting with him at a coffee shop. He walked up to Joshua, stared at him for a moment, then threw twenty five hundred dollars at him. He said "there, that should get you started." "When you find an apartment call me and let me know the address and I will send some of your things over." "Go, I never want to see you again," he said, and he turned his back on him and walked out the door.

It wasn't a surprise, he knew something like this would happen. He stayed at a hostel downtown San Fran for two days and then found a place. He had a friend call his father with the address and his stuff was there the next morning at seven am. That was the last of any contact with his father that Joshua ever had. Joshua raised his head to Astaroth and asked, "who killed my mother and where can I find him."

"His name is Keith Atkins," Astoroth said. "He lives in Los Angeles." "He continued to kill prostitutes for a few years and in an epiphany decided to become born again and be a follower of the Nazerene again." "He has become quite the citizen, helping street people and addicts find their way to the light so to speak." "Your priest has also mended his ways," Astaroth continued. "He was transferred to a new church in San Diego, about ten months after his incident with you." "He had some interactions, if you will, with a few other boys after you." "The arch diocese caught wind of it and swiftly transferred him."

"He too has seen the light of God and has changed his ways." "He still assists with masses and after a few years of therapy within the church, has become an advocate for the elderly and the disabled." "The ultimate hipocrate, I think," Astaroth said. "His God must be very proud." "He has never faced any retribution for what he has done."

"This is where you come in Joshua." "These men are working against our cause now." "In essence, their enlightenment is like spitting in the face of the master." "We want their souls, before there God decides that they have done enough good to deserve a second chance." "We want them dead and their bodies to lie sticking in the earth and their souls," Astaroth continued, "the dark one has a special place of suffering for them." "We want you to exact the revenge you mostly greatly deserve."

"This will provide two positive outcomes for Legion." "First, we will obtain their souls, and secondly it will bring you closer to us." "In addition to these two, there will be one other that the master has his eye on that you will be asked to dispose of," he said with a chuckle. "Who is it," Josh asked. "I don't have that disclosure yet," Astaroth replied.

"For your attention to these tasks and your soul of course, you will be granted more money then you could ever spend in one life time." "You will also be granted power and prestige over and above your fellow man, you will be envied and sought after," "You will be able to help gain other interests for Legion and the Dark one." "You will also have

ZACHARIAH LEHMANN

access to any female you want, you will not have to pursue them, they will pursue you." "This should satisfy you're lustful desires that we know run deep within side of you."

"But I only want Jade," Josh replied. "Well we will see what we can work out Josh," Astaroth said in dismissing fashion. "We know you quite fancy Jade, but she will not be part of your journey with us in the beginning." Josh turned to Jade and she looked very confused. She began to whimper and tears rolled down her face. "She will be assigned other tasks to help the cause," Astaroth said.

Joshua was dumbfounded. "Just because you say it will happen this way doesn't mean it will happen, I know you lie." "Josh I'm not lying to you, and if you speak to me common again like that, I will rip your heart out of your chest and eat it in front of her," looking at jade. "There is a contract that will be upheld," Astaroth said. "What I have said, I have forseen and will become reality." Josh had grown to love Jade very much. Actually it was beyond love, it was pure obsession. Whenever he looked in her eyes he thought he could see into her confusing but beautiful soul. He thought she was the only one he could trust.

"You will be assigned a few friends, those close to the cause and that who's futures depend on you success." "They will present themselves to you, and you will know them when you see them." Joshua thought for a moment then said, "so how does this work."

Chapter 10

"THERE'S NOTHING TO it," Astaroth said. "My associate will appear through the gate with the contract, you will sign, Crowley and I will witness and it will be done." "There's nothing to fear." "Everything that is promised will come to you." Joshua wanted wealth and to be powerful more than anything. But more than anything he craved power over his own life because he never had it. All his life he had been subservient and had been in vulnerable positions. Joshua looked Astaroth in the eyes and said, "let's get this done with."

Astaroth smiled and at that moment a large oak desk with a goat head emblem carved in the front and a pentagram on the top appeared within the cave. Then he saw a pant leg come through the portal. Jade just stood there wide eyed. Astaroth and the dragon and viper lowered their heads. Then the deity appeared.

He was the most beautiful man Joshua had ever seen. He had flowing black locks and huge black eyes. He looked at Astaroth, and the viper and dragon slithered away for the moment. He looked at Jade and she just dropped to her knees with her head down. "My name is Belial Josh, it's a pleasure to make your acquaintance."

Belial looked at Joshua, their eyes locked together, and Josh was mesmerized by the stare. Belial's hair was flowing even though there was no wind. Josh stood tall and stood his ground and showed no fear. He actually walked up to within 3 inches of the Belial and looked up.

Belial looked down and smiled, "you have a lot of balls my friend," he said with the sweetest voice you have ever heard. Belial then transformed into a Medusa head with vipers for hair, and roared and lunged at him. Joshua fell backwards on his ass. Then Belial changed back into his former shape, the beautiful man he was. "I can't let you get too comfortable, he said chuckling."

"I know what you want, and you know what you want," Belial said. "Just take it, Josh." "I have been watching you with great interest for some time." "Why is that," Joshua said, "I haven't really done anything of significance in my life." "But you are destined for greatness Josh," Belial said. "You're in the great position that if you give us the little that we ask, we will give what you desire during this life, and also protect you throughout eternity." Belial looked him in the eye and Josh matched his glance, trying not to show fear. Then all of the sudden, darkness.

Chapter 11

JOSHUA WAS IN an altered reality now. He was in a line up on a windy road that led to a cobblestone overpass in the distance. He looked around and it actually looked like Ireland, with the rolling green hills. But it was a terribly overcast day and there was a light fog about fifty feet about their heads, going up into the foothills. He looked straight up and in the center of the clouds was a huge black hole. It was swirling slowly yet there was still no wind, no voices or music. Josh looked ahead at the people that were in the line in front of him, and he saw a very social diverse crowd.

He saw only a few desolate people directly ahead of him in line, dressed in rags. They were the heathens. Whatever had happened to them in life, they we're now filled with pure hate and evil. They did not have the ability to feel compassion. They might have not actually caused physical harm to anyone, but there mere presence was a drain on the souls of others. They had the expression that they knew that their demons had come for them now. These people said nothing and had tears in their eyes, but were but seemed like they had accepted their fate.

They knew that this fate was inevitable, the final price for their sins. Next up was the well dressed, but obviously tainted narcissists. There were all complaining to each other about how they can't get out of this place, no matter which way they run the would always come back to the path that led to the overpass. The thing about their conversations was that they were always interrupting each other and trying to shout over each other to try to prove that their dilemma was more important than that of the others.

He looked ahead towards the front on the line and he couldn't believe his eyes. In the front he could see the murderers, child molesters and saddists, people who thrive on others pain and torture. They were all shouting "what the fuck, why am I here." "I'm innocent god damn it." "Nobody can prove anything of what I have done," they were saying.

A man among them in a dark cloak looked over and smartly said "they know the truth, what we have done." "It's not as in life, you can't hide what you want to hide." "That isn't the case here." "This is the end, my brothers and sisters." "I don't know what's going to happen after we get through that over pass, but I wish you well." "He gave them all a quick smile then quickly turned to face the front of the line.

But then Josh saw more people in front of that group. It was a party, a big party, but you couldn't hear them although they weren't too far away. Plus they looked like they were moving in slow motion. He saw flares from bonfires, and in the vapor above the top of the flames he saw bikers and politicians, the Mofia, and Ponzi sceamers who prayed on the elderly and destroyed their lives. "The human traffickers, the bikers and drug dealers who sold there spoils to children and ruined their lives. The Dictators, Totalitarianists and warlords who put their needs in front of their own people, and who made those people starve and suffer for their political gain.

Those who destroyed their own countries just in an attempt to retain their power. And others you couldn't really specify a demographic too, they were all partying hard, there were orgies and degradation. These were the worst of the worst. They were all yelling profanities with hand jesters like the horns of the devil.

It mostly looked like hippy and goth chicks riding on the shoulders of bikers and politicians. Josh saw a dee jay in the back to the right side and he could see the big stage and four, two story speakers surrounding him. He looked like a kid, maybe seventeen or eighteen. He was spinning like a mad man, and they were all reacting, but josh couldn't hear a thing. Or the others from that group. He heard nothing.

Out of the black hole and above the group of partiers became a swarm, maybe fifty or sixty of these flying creatures. They looked like the flying monkeys from the Wizard of Oz, but they were bigger. Same expression on their face though, an open mouth demonic smile, and black lifeless eyes like those of a great white shark. There wings were long, maybe a twelve foot span.

The crowd looked up as they gathered in the sky above them. They seemed worried for a moment, then went back to partying. The monkeys continued to swirl looking down at the crowd with their demonic smiles. The line kept on moving toward the overpass entrance, faster this time. Joshua could see a figure sitting in a lifeguard chair up ahead. He was hooded and was talking to the people entering the overpass.

All of the sudden the creatures in the sky swept down and started hunting. There was still no sound. They swooped down and picked off the people one by one with their talons and then took them up in the sky then flew down the entrance to the overpass and threw them in the air above the heads of those in line. They flew through the air and then it was as if they were sucked downwards at the end of the tunnel.

They all screamed like they knew what was happening. Joshua was now about fifty feet from the hooded figure in the stool. Some people in the line turned and looked at him with a look of utter hopelessness. Joshua just stared ahead, he didn't know what was going on either. He was going through the partiers now, and the monkeys continues to sweep down picking them up and throw them towards the ending of the tunnel. They flew through the air, looking to be in a lot of pain, screaming and wailing, but still Josh couldn't hear them.

Chapter 12

OSHUA WAS NOW about two people away from the hooded figure. He looked up at him but could not make out face. Just then he was right beside him. Joshua could now hear everything, he could hear the party, it was loud and everyone was screaming. But the loudest screams were those being picked up by the flying monkeys. The monkeys were still expressionless picking them up in the air and throwing through the tunnel towards the end, where they were sucked down towards the ground. Joshua then heard a "hey," from above.

The figure on the stool was now looking down at him. It was now his turn. "Pay no attention to that group, you are all in the same situation." "Name," the figure yelled at him. He looked up and said "Joshua, Joshua Cain." "Oh let's see here," the hooded figure said. "Oh yes Cain, wonderful name by the way, sent by Belial, a visitor," he said with a chuckle. "Wow we haven't had a visitor in quite some time."

"I remember the Nazarene came down for a visit once." "We all made it quite known he wasn't welcome." "He made his way through the line picking out some people as we all watched, he lead his flock the other way." "The rest of the crowd begged to go as well, but to no avail." "They just begged for his mercy but could not move and the Nazarene would not look back."

"But anyways, you are no savior, Joshua Cain." "You are just here for the ride." "And believe me," the figure said, "I will give you the full sense of your environment," he said as a dragon's head charged out from the head of the cloak, with a huge smile on it's face. It disappeared back into the clock and then the beast said, "move along you prick!"

The line kept moving, quicker this time. He was now entering the overpass. He saw figures on each side in the tunnel. They were just black silhouettes, because there was only a very limited amount of red light emanating from the end of the overpass.

Joshua looked ahead and now he could see a large well at the end of the tunnel. He saw a outline of a Primantis about a story and a half tall. Some were jumping into the well. One guy even did a backwards swan dive off the edge of the well into the hole, and flames emanated as soon as he was out of site. The black Primantis looked at Joshua with huge green eyes and then Josh heard and felt a pulsing sensation. Josh covered his ears but the pulsing did not go away. The pulsing faded and Joshua looked up and he saw he was about twelfth in line to the well. But he was pushed forward and the line was moving up quickly.

He looked up and the Primantis lunged backward, he was huge when you were up close. It raised his spiked tentacle and impaled the guy right in front of Josh. The guy was half in the air impaled by the tentacle spear. He look down at Josh with a face of utter despair. And then the Primantis threw him violently and quickly into the well. There was a small fire burst but that was it.

Josh stepped up to the well and looked up. The Primantis was staring back with those green eyes and they connected. Then the pulsing started again while their eyes were locked. This time about twenty times worse. Josh whole body started pulsing. Their eyes were still locked. The pain was intensifying. He looked beyond the well at the end of the tunnel and it was an empty void. But there were light flickers in it just as if an old TV had just broken.

Josh shook his head, then and was free from the pulsing for just one moment. He took two giant steps and leap for all his life into the well. On the way down he heard the Primantis screeching. He fell right through the well, screaming and there was intense heat below him. He was hurtling toward a rock floor. Then he stopped and was levitating.

Chapter 13

THE ROCK FLOOR opened up again and there was some light that seemed to be earthly like. He floated down to another rock floor and looked up and he was facing Belial, this time they were face to face with one another.

"So you saw the bad side, the transition from the living to the damned," Belial started. "Believe me, you'd be going there if you didn't sign your soul over anyway," he said with a serious stern look. "You ok my boy." Joshed chocked a little bit cleared his throat and said, "just fine, thanks." "You won't have to endure any of that on the day of judgement if you cooperate and serve the dark lord."

"Are you willing to sign your soul to Lucifer Joshua," Belial said looking perplexed as if he didn't know what Joshua's answer would be. "So you can avoid this tragic eternity of burning, suffering and total helplessness."

"I am," Joshua said, "as long as you fulfill your promises as well." Not to worry, Belial said. "Look over the terms and conditions," Belial said and handed him a scroll sealed with wax. Joshua broke the wax and unraveled the paper.

He looked over the document carefully. Everything was in place as discussed, and there was already a signature at the bottom it said Lucifer in large Cryptic letters. "We will have to take Jade with us, she's not going to hellfire, but she simply cannot distract you on your mission." "But you will see her again, I promise you that," Belial said.

"How long do I have with her," Josh asked as he looked at Jade. "Maybe tomorrow, maybe not," Belial said with a smile. "I'm pleased because I know this is killing you inside." "I know you have never loved any so much in your life but get over it, it's just for a short time and it's for the best." Josh looked into Belial's eyes. Belials face lite up. "Nice, very nice, I can feel your hate," he said with a big smile.

Josh stared with a scary look of hate. They locked eyes for about three seconds which felt like an hour and then josh broke the connection and looked away towards the cave wall. "If that's the way it has to be, I'll wait for her." "Love is for the weak Josh, women are to be used and abused." "Josh you will have any woman you want, you won't even have to pursue them, they will come to you, just not Jade for the time being."

"The Master believes she would be a source of weakness for you and would make you stray from the path chosen for you." Joshua nodded and sat in the chair in front of the desk. Belial was in front of the desk and signed backwards to him. Joshua looked Belial in the eyes and Belial said with his sweet voice and a smile, "do not fear my boy, it will all turn out in the end."

Joshua pondered for about another minute with Belial still grinning and his face glowing like he was angelic. He put the feather ink and paper and signed his name. "We will be seeing each other sooner than you think, Joshua." Astaroth then came up beside Belial and said, "my lord." Belial looked at him and nodded and Astaroth signed as a witness.

Then through the cave opening, Crowley appeared in human form in a catholic priest dressing with blood smeared across the white collar and an upside down crucifix which looked to have feces on it around his neck. He smiled with a big smile on his face and signed as well. "Best decision you ever made Joshua, you will have wealth and power beyond your belief," Crowley said. He looked at Joshua with a small chuckle then disappeared again into the darkness. Belial smiled at Josh, turned and said "I will be seeing you then friend," snapped his fingers and jumped into the portal.

Astaroth took a step back and looked at Josh and said "good choice, I'm proud of you." He mounted the dragon and said, "we will be in communication soon." Astaroth then turned the dragon and disappeared into the portal. Then the portal imploded into itself with Joshua and jade standing there with just the light of the lantern.

Right away Josh felt there was something missing inside of him. "Wow," Josh said, "that was pretty intense." "You handled yourself very well," Jade said, still crying and sniffling from the news. "I know good things will happen to you soon," Jade said. "I've never wanted a drink and toke so bad in my life," Josh said. "Let's get home gorgeous, while we still have time together."

They gathered there stuff and started back to the car. It was pitch black now so they kept the lantern going to read the compass. Crowley was gone and wasn't following them anymore. It was so calm and peaceful in the woods now. They made it back to the car and took off towards home.

Chapter 14

THEY MADE IT back to his place and Joshua cracked a Strongbow and got the bong ready. Jade poured herself a glass of wine, smiled at him and said, "light it up, light it up." Joshua put a nice piece of hash in there and some weed, and they smoked and drank for a couple hours reminiscing about that nights events and there union up until that point.

"I'll miss you more than any other person I have known except for John," she said beginning to sob uncontrollable. "I'll will miss you more than anything too, I really do love you," and he grabbed and held her and he did not want to let go.

They had been smoking and drinking for a couple of hours then Jade startled him on the couch, looked him deep in the eyes then sucked on his earlobe and whispered in his ear, "make love to me josh, I love you." "I love you too," he said.

They went upstairs into the bedroom and they made passionate love like never before. When Josh came it was pure extacy and jade came at the same time and she was screaming like a banshee. Josh then rolled over and said still panting, "Wow, that was great timing." Jade nodded in agreement as they both tried to catch their breath.

"We'll deal with whatever the day brings tomorrow, I just hope we're together still," he said sadly. "Josh, I'm so scared to sleep hun, I don't want to lose you, I just got you and now their taking you away from me." "You mean so much to me now, you're the only person in my life, you know I don't have any family, no real friends, no kids, you really are the only person in my life." "We're two soulmate misfits that the devil brought together and now we don't have control of our own destinies," Josh said. "Your my absolute best friend and lover, I hope we won't be apart very long."

"We're the best drinking and drugging buddies," he said with a laugh, "who are there to accomplish one goal, to forget everything and make the pain go away." "My life has meaning with you." "Before there was such emptiness, now I'm going to have to go through that again." "I love you so much," Jade said again looking in his eyes. She kissed him softly on the cheek. There was a two minute paused while they thought about their situation, trying to come up with a way out, but they knew there were none.

"So what do you think, are they going to take me and keep me somewhere well you do what you have to do, or will I be here and you're gone." "Josh I have something to tell you, it's a little bit important." She paused again for about two minutes and started laughing and crying at the same time. "I'm sorry, I don't know how to express myself when I'm upset as she wiped the tears away from her eyes." "She put her head down and then looked up at him, "all I have to say is there is a reason why where so perfect together."

"But I can't tell you till I see you again," Jade said and then closed her eyes and started smiling. "And I know I WILL see you again." "It will either be in this world or," she said so sweetly looking out the skylight pointing at the stars, "in some other dimension out there."

"I know, it will be here Jade, I know I will see you soon." "You and I belong together." "And when I see you again," Josh said with a big smile, "we're going to get married and have a bunch of puppies." "Puppies," she said laughing. "That's just my stupid word for kids," Josh said with a smile. "Let's take a chance now and try to sleep and just hope we're still together tomorrow." "Hope's a pretty powerful thing," Josh said with a half smile.

"Ok," she said starting to cry again. Josh lied back in bed with a huge knot in his stomach. He was staring at the skylight and Jade grabbed him gently by the back of the head and turned his head so they were starring each other in the eye with no fear of either one of them pulling away. They both stayed like that for about forty five seconds. Josh just got mesmerized by her eyes, and then started to see visions. Josh couldn't make them out but he knew they were violent, very violent. He blinked and pulled away.

She grabbed him by the back of the head and pulled him in again and gave Josh the sweetest most innocent kiss he had ever experienced. "Good night," she said and with a frown on her face and sniffling, as she rolled over and curled up against him in bed. "I want to go down to the park by the water tomorrow, there's going to be a free concert." "And I want the real Joshua tomorrow so no drinking." "That's what we're doing, it's a done deal," and she rolled over. Josh was having some tremors, a bit from the alcohol but mostly from his terrifying fear.

Chapter 15

BANG, BANG, BANG...BANG, BANG. Jade woke and sat straight up, sweet pouring. BANG, BANG. It was the cupboards in the kitchen, they were slamming open and shut. She then heard a loud pig squeal. She looked up at the wall where the light was coming in from the street and saw the silhouette of Azazel. He was making obscene gestures with his tongue and she could tell that snout and horns from a mile away.

"YOU'RE NOT SUPPOSED TO BE HERE THIS SOON, GO AWAY," she screamed furiously into the air. Another loud pig squeal. She turned and grabbed Josh to wake him. She didn't know why he wasn't awake already. He was on his side with his back towards her. "Josh," she yelled and grabbed him by the shoulder. She pulled him over and he was on his back. When she looked Josh had no face, just a blank piece of skin with the outline of a nose and mouth. No eyes.

He started with small convulsions, and they quickly got worse. With no face and with the body jumping up into the air with limbs flailing. The body flung upwards and hit the ceiling three times with loud bangs. Then the body floated down to Jade's level and the face turned toward jade. Josh's face still looked like just skin but it now had eyes. Not really eyes but jagged holes in the face, and there was nothingness behind the eyes. Black, shiny black.

She saw a spec of what looked like a silver comet go through one of the eyeholes. Jade was in a different dimension. She was caught with small pieces of her reality but the power flowed mostly from a different realm. She heard the squeal again. She looked up at the wall again and the silhouette of Azazel was smiling at her. Josh was sitting beside her in the corner of the room, no face but looking at her. He looked like a cartoon character but in the real world.

It was like watching like watching a TV rerun over and over quickly. Jade had never been so horrified in her life. The cabinets started banging again quickly then they stopped suddenly. "Squeeaal," she heard ringing in her ears and that the end of the squeal she heard "Jaaadddeee," with a loud screech. She was now looking around looking for any other way out. She saw nothing, Josh was still bobbing up and down. He now looked like a blur he was spazming so quickly. She heard something moving on their dresser across the room. As soon as she turned to look she was hit hard in the nose with the portable phone that was on the dresser.

She felt shooting pains shooting up into her brains. Her nose was seriously bleeding. She was bleeding all over herself. There was no sound in the apartment. Then she heard with a deep lifeless voice a long drawn out "JADE," but it was not an exterior noise. Azazel was now in her mind. That cabinets started banging really hard now breaking the silent of the outside world. She heard two more loud squeals from Azazel that ripped through her brain like a train wreck.

She got up and grabbed some clothes from the dresser, looked over at Josh and he just looked like a blur. He looked like he was turning into a black hole, just voidness. She began to rush towards the door, the cabinets were just pounding in unison now it was so loud. She got to the front door and went through. She closed the door and all the cabinets stopped, and it seemed that the outside world again had no sound. Then another squeal in her head. It was so loud that she dropped to her knees and covered her ears as if that would help her. "Jade, come on down," Azazel said in his price is right voice.

"There's no way to fight this," she thought just mentally giving up. "There is no way out unless I face him." She started down the stairs and started praying with her voice but could hear nothing. She started praying with her inner voice, "God, Lord Jesus, please help me in my time of need. I realize I left you but I know I am a good person and I really need you now," she pleaded.

"What a feeble, pathetic attempt at salvation from a dead God," Azazel said to her in her head. She reached the door and slowly went through, starting to sob. She looked up, and saw Azazel. He had two

ZACHARIAH LEHMANN

huge black dogs with him. "You couldn't let me have ONE fucking day with him," she shouted but no noise came out of her.

She looked at him again but he looked like a mirage about to disappear, just black figures in beneath a blood red sky. Then in her head she heard "Shut Your Mouth You Filthy Sow." "Do want another phone to the head, because I can arrange that." "GET OVER HERE," he shouted with literally steam emanating from his body.

She stood there stunned for a moment and thought, "is this the Really, Real world, of course not." "It's not at all." She regained her composure and started slowly towards them. They were on the other side of the street. There were no cars or people on the street. She felt and heard a gust of cold wind hit her.

Then the squeal again, it was high pitched but it wasn't in her head. She could hear now. She was looking down again because she couldn't stand the putrid site of him, but she looked up. She got slowly closer and he began to talk. "Why do you pray to that useless Nazarene." "He hasn't done anything good for over two thousand years."

"I consider him and his father dead a long time ago." "You belong to us now my dear," he said sweetly to her. She finally had reached him. The two dogs started walking away leaving the two of them.

Azazel violently grabbed her head and pulled her in so they were pretty much face to face. He licked his pig lips again and with his left hand, went quickly down her pants and started fingering her vagina. Then he brought his fingers to his pig nose and started snorting and sniffing. "Oh nice," he said calmly and with a smile on his face. "You fucked him last night, I can smell." "Well you are going to be very sexually active where you're going with us," he said with a childish giggle.

Then he licked the blood from her nose with his snake tongue and had a satisfied look on his face. He smiled at her and again grabbed her by the back of the head and threw her by the hair in the other direction, facing down the road. "Walk quickly now," he snorted. She was wincing and trying to fix her hair. He was such a vile and disgusting creature. She then looked down the road and started walking. There were still no people or cars on the street. It felt like the barometer had dropped so low. It was hard for her to breath.

Up ahead on the left side of the road she saw a vacant lot between the houses on the left hand side. She walked even faster to get ahead of them a bit. Azazel shouted out, "take the path through the lot and up over the hills into the fire my dear." Jade thought he was talking about the blood red sky. Just then she heard from over the hills sounds of screaming. They were faint, but they were horribly tortured soulless screams. "Stop at the top of the mountain if you get too far ahead," Azazel said. "The sheer horror of what's over there will stop you anyways," he said with that stupid smile again. She continued to walk ahead of them and followed the path like she was told.

Chapter 16

THE NEXT DAY **Josh** awoke and rolled over to cuddle but Jade wasn't beside him. He remembered what happened the day before. He put his head in his hands and he began to weep. "Not even today with her, that's pretty fucking cheap to take her the same night like that." He didn't hear anything in the night, he slept completely soundly. Tomorrow Wendy, by concrete blonde was playing on the radio. He started listening to the lyrics, [I told the priest don't count on any second coming God got his ass kicked the last time he came down here slumming, he had the balls to die and then forgive us no I don't wonder why I wonder what he thought it would get us, hey hey goodbye, tomorrow Wendy's GOING TO DIE.]

He didn't just love Jade, he had a need inside of him that he had to be with her. It was an unnatural feeling. Josh fought it the best he could. Joshua's hatred for God grew exponentially then. He saw God as weak, with no real power over anything. Not able to do anything about what is going on in the world. God didn't save Jade from the evil. He wondered if God ever did have any power on Earth. It seemed that in his life, evil was definitely the greater influence. God was just a fading figure in the rear view mirror.

"Fuck this sucks so bad," he said to himself still whimpering. He got up took a shower and got ready, and he was off to the liquor store and his dealer. He was back at the house in about an hour and got right back into the drinking and smoking.

About an hour later he got a call on his cell. He was half expecting it to be Jade telling him where she was. "Hello," he said anxiously. A male voice was on the other line. "Hi can I speak with Mr. Joshua please." "No, that's my first name." "My name's Craig Skiles, I'm with a company called DNL, you had forwarded your resume to us about two weeks ago." Josh had been continuously sending out resumes for the past three months trying to get a day job. He was really looking to get out of the bar scene.

I've been a little busy the past couple of weeks and I finally got a chance to look at your resume," Craig said. "I'd really like to meet up with you Josh and discuss a position we are hiring for." "I think you might be a good fit with us." "Can you come in and talk with me tomorrow." "For sure," Josh said, "what time would you like me there."

"How about two," Craig said. "Sounds perfect," Josh said. "Do you know where we are." "Is the address on your website." Yeah it sure is, or Google map it," Craig said. "Oh, I'll get there for sure," Josh said eagerly. "When you get to security downstairs, just let them know you have a meeting with me at two." Sounds great Mr. Skiles, I'm looking forward to meeting you." "OK, have a good night and I'll see you tomorrow." "Thanks," Josh said and hung up.

"Wow," Josh thought, this was happening a little too quickly. He was still mourning the loss of Jade. He got on his laptop. He went to DNL website. They were a progressive importing and exporting company. They dealt in fossil fuels, lumber, weapons parts and all kinds of food distribution.

They were 24 on the fortune 500 list of companies and where listed as one of the top 50 employers to work for in the US. Not too bad he thought to himself. Josh somehow thought because of the contract that this was going to work out whether the interview went well or not. He read the website and was fully impressed, then grabbed another Strongbow and the bong and started hard again on his substance abuse. He couldn't keep Jade out of his mind. It had been less than a day but he missed her so much. He ironed his clothes and watched TV for about another hour and a half and then passed out on the couch.

Chapter 17

HE NEXT DAY he woke up with not too bad of a hangover and had a few Strongbow's just to get a little of the dog that bit him into him. He left about one O'clock, it wouldn't take him to long to get down there. He got to DNL at about one forty, got to the security desk and told them he had an appointment to see Mr. Skiles. They let him right through and said the office was on the twenty ninth floor.

He boarded the elevator and made his way up. He walked out of the elevator and the secretary looked up with a big small on her face and said "Mr. Joshua very nice to meet you, Craig's just finishing something up, he'll be with you in a quick," "I'm Sadie, she said. She was an absolutely gorgeous She was green eyed and had gorgeous long red hair.

"Why do you all call me Mr. Joshua," he asked her. "That's your name silly, she said with a big smile," "That what we're calling you here anyways." He went to sit down She kept on looking over at him and giving him a quick smile. "Craig's really looking forward to meeting you," she said. "Same here," Josh said.

Craig's office door opened, "Come on in Josh," he said loudly. Josh entered the office and Craig said, "have a seat sir." He was a shorter man with glasses and blonde hair. "It's great to meet you Craig," "Same here," Craig said. "Wow, you have a great view," Josh said looking at the view of the bay. "Yeah, it's not too bad at all."

"So the job I had you in mind for you Mr. Joshua is junior director southwest operations." "The senior director's name is Brad Richardson." "He's a great guy, I thing you'll get along well." "He can show you all the ins and outs of the job when you come on board." "He's also retiring in six months, so my plan is for him to groom you into his successor in that time."

"It's not rocket science, it's pretty simple stuff as long as you stay focused and you're a quick study." "The position starts at 300000/annum." "Does it sound like something you'd be interested in Mr. Joshua," Craig said. "Absolutely," Josh answered.

"To tell you the truth I was applying for more of an entry level position, but this is unbelievable." "Well Josh, I'm not offering you this position based on your resume." "We have some mutual friends that think you would be a perfect fit." "Our friend Astaroth has nothing but good things to say about you, and when he speaks I listen," Craig said. "He is my master just like yours, and we always take care of our own."

"All you have to do is do a good job for me and we will take care of you." "Do you speak with Astaroth on a regular basis," Josh asked. "Just when the need arises, he's a pretty busy guy," Craig said smiling. "Belial is third in command down there Josh." "Most never see him." "I'm astounded to know he was there to recruit you." "There is something special about you Mr. Joshua, and we are going to find out what it is, me and you," he said with a trusting smile like he truly did care about him.

"That's another thing Josh, Astaroth has asked me to bring you into our coven." "He wants you to have a complete understanding of who you are now." "We meet regularly on the first full moon of every month at the reservation park." "I will sponsor you into the coven." "It'll be a week before the coven meets again so there's much time to talk about that." "In the mean time you should take a look at this," Craig handed him a copy of the Complete Book of Spells, Ceremonies, and Magic.

"Study this for next week, try some spells and we'll discuss it again at the Sabbat." Focus on chaos and destruction Mr. Joshua." "Sounds good," Josh said a little freaked out. "So what is it Wednesday today, so Mr. Joshua why don't you start on Monday that will give you time to tie up some lose ends."

"I can't tell you how much I appreciate this," Josh said. "Anytime my boy, your family now and remember we take care of our own." "I'll see you here eight thirty Monday, have a great weekend," Craig said not looking at him and practicing his putting stroke.

Josh smiled at Sadie the receptionist as he was leaving. "Looking forward to seeing you on Monday and at the Sabbat next week," "Stick close to me at the there and ill treat you real well." "I love fresh meat,"

ZACHARIAH LEHMANN

she said with an evil little giggle. "Sounds good darlin, I'll see you next week."

As he was leaving, one of the building security guards said. "I here you will be joining us on Monday, Mr. Skiles just sent down the world." "Do you mind if we take your picture for the security badge." "Not at all," Josh said. "Do you need my last name," Josh asked anxiously. "No sir, your Mr. Joshua when you're here." "Of course," Josh said with a laugh. "Pop in before you head upstairs Monday and it'll be ready for you." "Thank you sir," Josh said with a smile and walked out. "Have a good rest of the weekend," one of them said. "You as well," Josh said as he left the building with a big smile on his face.

He left the building and shouted "yes," as he pumped his fist. He never thought something could happen like this in his life, and so soon. It was three o'clock and Sergei would be at the pub by now. He decided to go over and tell him he was leaving. He had nothing against Sergei, they were good friends and he felt guilty he would have to leave such short notice.

He walked into the pub and there was the same fifteen day regulars that had been for years. Then he saw Sergei. "To what do I owe this pleasure during the day sir," "you're a night crawler aren't you." I got to talk to you for a quick Sergei, you got a couple of minutes," Josh asked. "For sure, sir can I offer you a tasty beverage," Sergei said ready to pour the Strongbow tap. "Absolutely," Josh said. "Step into my office," Sergei said as they went and sat down by the pool tables.

"Sergei, I have to give my notice." "I'm so sorry man." Sergei hung his head for a minute and said, "I knew this was going to happen." "You're a big fish in a really fucking small pond Joshua." "I'm going to be working for a big company that offered me six digits to start," Josh said with a smile. "Holy shit," Sergei said, "you really hit the pot of gold my boy." "I can work up until Saturday night, I know you'll find someone good, why don't you bump Matt up into my spot."

"I think I'll do that, I'm gonna miss you brother." "Don't be a stranger now that you're the big corporate sucker." "I'll say goodbye to the boys for you Josh," Sergei said chuckling, referring to the fags. "Hey Sarah, could you bring over another pitcher of Strongbow." "Sure boss." All three of them poured a pint and Sergei clanged Josh's glass, "Cheers to brighter skies ahead." "Yes sir," Josh replied.

"Well, I'm truly happy for you my friend, I'd say come back and see up but don't show your face in here again," Sarah said with fierce eyes, half jokingly, half not. "You're growing up now Josh, don't look back," Sarah said as she gave him a big hug. "If I see you here again ill kick the shit out of you," she said as they were both laughing.

"I'll miss you as well," Josh said, "but I got all your guy's numbers." "I'll be in touch." "Not too many before you go to work at this place, I know you sir," Sergei said. "I'll try not to," Joshua said. "See you soon folks," and Josh finished his pint and left. "That couldn't have gone better," Josh said to himself. He jumped in the firebird and made his way home.

ZACHARIAH LEHMANN

Chapter 18

JOSH FINISHED OFF his last shift on Saturday and they had a great send off for him after hours at the bar. Even some of the regulars got to stay. It was endless Strongbow that night for Joshua and everyone eventually filed out of the place around five am. Josh stumbled out of the bar, being carried by Barbie, one of the waitresses and she directed him to his car. Josh decided he would have to leave the firebird there for the night, but it would be safe.

"Barbie you're the best for taking me home, I love you," Josh said slurring. "So are you gonna come in for a few more drinks when we get there," Josh said with a stupid smile on his face. "Sounds good," Barbie said. Josh had always been attracted to her, a gorgeous brunette with and huge breasts and an ass that wouldn't quit.

She had been in a relationship for three years but had broken it off with her boyfriend about two weeks ago. "She was nice and vulnerable," Josh thought to himself. Now she was fucking everything that was good looking and showed her any attention. He spoke to himself in the car under his breath, "Astaroth, please let me stay hard for this one."

"Who are you talking to," Barbie asked looking a little annoyed. "Oh, no one, I was just babbling." "So what happened with Dex," Josh asked referring to her ex. She kept on badmouthing him until they got back to his place. She helped him inside and threw him on the couch. Josh had a really nice bottle of wine, Grey Monk, late harvest 1995, and he uncorked that in honor of her presence, and him getting his dick wet.

Josh talked to Barbie about Jade, not getting into details about what happened but shed tears when he talked about her. Barbie sympathized saying "it sucks when they just leave like that." "I was in love with her,"

Josh said looking lost, "but I gotta move on." "Absolutely," Barbie said as she moved over and started stroking him with a smile on her face. "I think we should finish this bottle and then proceed to the bedroom," Josh said. She nodded still smiling. They talked about his new job for the next little while but Josh didn't have too much to tell, he really didn't know the job himself.

Then they went up to the bedroom and got down to business. When they got to the bedroom, they started ripping each other's clothes off. He went down on her and she squealed and moaned. Josh was always good at that. He always got his fingers involved. She eventually sat up and pushed him over, which wasn't very hard, and went down on him. It took about ten minutes until he was hard and then josh started missionary with her feet around her head. After a few minutes of that, he commanded her to get on all fours.

Doggy was the only way he was going to cum. He had her by the hips and was pounding hard from behind. He lasted about six minutes and then came inside of her holding her hips and her ass close to him while he ejaculated inside of her. Josh then rolled over and passed out cold.

"That's it, no fucking cuddling," Barbie questioned Josh with no response from him. "Fuck," she said and kissed him on the forehead as she got dressed and left.

Chapter 19

THE NEXT DAY he was up around three and his stomach was killing him. He could barely see, but he could move slowly. He wasn't surprised Barbie was gone, just another woman who left him behind. He would probably never see her again. Despite what he said to Sergei, he had no intentions of hanging out at the bar. He had started a new life, this was a new beginning for him.

He reluctantly took a shower and made his way on the streetcar to the bar to pick up the firebird. Thank God it was still there, and he got in and made his way to the party store for another twelve of Strongbow. This would get him through the day. He went to the grocery store as well and picked up a roasted chicken and a potato salad for dinner. He should be ok for Monday as long as he ate and drank his can. He spent a leisurely day on the couch, watched the Giant's game on TV.

At around nine that night, he ironed his shirt, got his black cotton suit out of the closet and tied his tie for the next day. He took a shower and shaved and it would probably only take him fifteen minutes to leave in the morning. He got to bed around ten thirty and had the best sleep of his life.

Chapter 20

H E WOKE UP at eight feeling good. He got ready in about 10 minutes, then walked down the road and hopped on the streetcar. He got to the DNL building around eight fifteen. There was a bit of a line up at the security desk but one of the guards waved him ahead. "Mr. Joshua," he said, "hope you had a pleasant weekend." "Here is your security badge, and here's an extra just in case." "Go right through, Mr. Skiles is expecting you." "Thanks very much," Josh said walking towards the elevator.

He made his way up to the office and Sadie was there smiling. "Hello Mr. Joshua, how was your weekend." "Uneventful," Josh said still hung over, "how about you." "It was good, I didn't get into trouble for a change." "That's always a good thing," Josh said and they both smiled. Craig walked out and said "Hey Josh, right on time, I like that, come on in and meet Brad." Yeah for sure, Josh said as he entered the office. Brad stood up and shook Josh's hand. He looked in his late fifty's in an impeccable black suit. He had grey hair, black eyes and inviting smile.

"Hey, very nice to meet you," Josh said. "It sounds like we'll be spending a lot of time together the next six months." "Yes we will," Craig responded, "we have a few things to go over before I'm gone." "Please call me Brad, even though I'm retiring I don't want to feel like an old man," he said with a chuckle. "Not a problem Brad." "So let's head down and I'll show you your office."

"There's lots of computer passwords and email we have to get set up. "Let's do it," Josh said. They were in the elevator and brad said, "this isn't too stressful a job Josh, once you're in, your in." Just stay focused and I'm sure you'll be fine when you take over for me." "You'll have to get on the phone with the tech guys and get everything set up." Josh got to his office and Brad said, "the tech number is on your desk, give them a call and I hope I'll see you in a couple hours." "Hope it doesn't take the whole day," Brad said laughing.

Joshua got on the phone and four hours of frustration later was finished. He went over to Brad's corner office and he was on the phone, so he politely waited just outside. Brad finished his conversation about ten minutes later and waved Josh in.

"Well that didn't take too long," Brad said with a chuckle. "Thanks for your patience, I know that's a real pain in the ass." "So let's get down to business," Brad started, "It's almost the end of the day and I want to let you out a bit early today so we won't cover too much." Brad started to help Josh with analyzing the reports. "So I'm going to shadow you for the couple weeks and then we'll make a corporate announcement that you're on board, then you'll start picking up some of my slack." Brad was teaching Josh how to navigate through the back office tools and then it was time to go.

"Well you look like you're going to catch on just fine." "We'll start again tomorrow." "Craig wants to see you before you leave, so just pop your head in before you take off." "Thanks very much Brad, I'm really excited about this opportunity and being able to learn from you." "Stop kissing my ass and get out of here," Brad said with a chuckle.

Joshua took the stairs up to the next floor where Craig's office was and Sadie was at she desk. "So how was the first day Josh." "Great," Craig waved him into the office. "The Sabbat's tomorrow so I'll swing by pick you up about eight after work." "I have your address." "Sounds good Craig, I'll see you tomorrow."

"You bet, Sadie's really excited your coming," Craig said, "you must have made a good impression." "Nice," Josh said with a smile. "Alright go home and take it easy and we'll see you bright and early." "Sounds good Craig, have a good night as well." "Oh, I'll be here for another three hours, but thanks anyways," Craig said chuckling. He walked out and Sadie said with a big smile, "see you tomorrow sweetie." He smiled back and said, "Night," as he proceeded to the elevator.

Chapter 21

JOSH GOT HOME from work on Tuesday. It had been a pretty uneventful day. He cracked a Strongbow and thought that he would have to be careful tonight. He didn't want to be too fucked up. He started to read the book of spells Craig gave him. He also had the encyclopedia of demons and demonology. He wasn't actually going to try any spells today, just learn about the major Demons, and how they could help him. But his allegiance was absolutely with Astaroth, Azazel, and most of all, Belial.

Belial had keep his word and things were really working out. He felt power over his life that he never had felt before, but still felt the voidness of Jade not being with him. He wondered when he would see her again. Weeks, months, years. She would not leave his mind when he was alone. He had to see her again, but decided he wouldn't press it with Belial.

But he really enjoyed the respect he got at work and from the other people in his life, and even strangers. He wasn't a dick to them, he was also respectful of them as well. Josh was looking at curses, he had no one he really wanted to curse, except his ex from a few years ago. She had left him for another man and she and he would get great pleasure by calling Josh up and mocking him because she was gone. She was an absolute whore, but he decided not to because he learned to put a curse on someone, everything could come back on you tenfold.

Chapter 22

I T WAS ABOUT seven thirty, Josh got dressed and took a shower. He got one more Strongbow and slammed it down. He had actually paced himself pretty good throughout the evening. It was five to eight and he went out to the driveway for a smoke. He was getting really nervous. "New start for everything," he said to himself.

Craig pulled up in what looked to be brand new black BMW seven series. He was dressed in black and was on the phone and waved him into the car. Josh jumped in, gave him a nod, and they were off down the hill.

The city looked huge from that view. Craig started being aggressive on the phone and getting really pissed with the woman he was talking too. Josh had only known Craig as being nice to him so he was a little surprised. "JUST DO IT," Craig screamed as he hung up the phone. "Fucking women eh, when you can't live with them, next thing is to cut their fucking heads off," and he and Josh both laughed. "Listen, I know you're nervous," and slapped him on the thigh. "I was too." "Just remember you're protected." "You've been to these things before, just not with us."

"The coven tends to notice new bee's right away, so expect some attention." "But we're there, so no worries." "Me and Astaroth have got some great expectations for you my son," as he slapped his thigh again, leaving it stinging this time. So a little birdie told me you signed your pack with Astaroth and Belial, you'll have to give me the details. Josh looked perplexed, then started to tell his condensed version. Right before the end of his tale, he two got to the park. "Man, I want to hear the end of that," Craig said, "but we gotta jet."

Josh could here in the distance that the Sabbat had started. Craig yelled "come on, we're late," and started running. "Here's your robe, Craig threw it to him, "we'll be sure to put them on before we get there." "Fair enough," Josh said and took off towards the fire up ahead in the distance. Craig chased and caught up with him.

Craig was ahead of him and stopped and bent over and said, "stop, stop, stop." Joshua let up, bent over and started trying to catch his breath. He wasn't in shape at all anymore. "Let's put the robes on." They put them on over their clothes and were tying the ropes around their waists. "Lets do this," Craig said with a sly smile. Craig motioned to him and they both started walking towards the crowd.

Chapter 23

THEY GOT THEMSELVES together and started looking for Brad and Sadie. Craig was stopping every five seconds and addressing someone and making a triangle with his two hands and then walking away. Suddenly Sadie turned around and said with excitement, "Brad, there here." "Josh, Craig," Sadie shouted. Craig looked over but was still talking to someone. Josh went over they hugged and she said, "wow Josh, you're in for some fun tonight". Brad shook Josh's hand with a big smile and said, "glad you could make it."

Then the ritual started. There were three men in robes on top of the make shift stage. On the stage was the Alter. There was a severed goat's head on the alter with it's eyes cut out. There was a crucifix on the alter facing the crowd. They walked to the front and started spitting on the crucifix. One of them urinated on it and turned to crowd for a reaction and everyone started cheering. One woman smeared her own menstral blood on it. Just then, two other men lead a naked woman in her twenties out. She was screaming and begging, "please don't do this, I want to live please, please don't do this".

The three men grabbed her as she struggled, and tied her down to ropes attached to the Alter. She was screaming and weeping "No, No please, I can't die this way." Then one of the men covered her mouth and then raised one finger to his mouth and she was quiet, undoubtedly understanding her fate.

The three took turns mounting her on the Alter and raping her, while spitting on her and slapping her. Finally the High priest grabbed a dagger on the Alter and began speaking. "Satan and all you're minions, god and our master, we all hear you and know we have a place with you if we are obedient." "We offer this sacrifice to you, she is a virgin, and we will feed from her in honor of your name."

At that point the crowd started chanting a demonic prayer that Josh did not recognize, he stayed silent. The girl was still struggling with the ropes to no avail. The men were standing in a trinity formation, with the leader in the front holding the dagger. He began speaking Latin, lifted the dagger above his head and jabbed it into her chest. Her head shot up but her body could not move. The warlock then took a sword from the Alter. The blade was glistening from the light of the fire. The other men untied her and threw her down on her knees in front of him.

"Go fuck yourself and your mother," the girl screamed and split on him." He let out a load roar, and brought the sword up. The blade came down and cut her head clean off, to the roar of the crowd. The severed head had rolled a few feet to the side, and the body fell to the stage and was convulsing.

The warlock went over and picked up the severed head and proceeded to cut the eyes out. He placed them in a small black pouch and put them aside for himself on the Alter. He then went over the body, bent down and started eating the innerds out off the head cavity. Josh thought it was absolutely repulsive. Like dogs, the other two started slurping up the blood from the puddle of blood beside her. After about a minute her body stopped convulsing.

Then the high priest took some of the blood and put it on the five points of the Pentagram on the floor of the make stage as the blood sacrifice given to Satan. The three then took the head and body and tossed them to the crowd. Josh couldn't see what was going on, but the crowd swarmed in.

Just then Craig and Brad grabbed Josh's arm. "What are you guy's doing." "Don't worry, it's just part of the ritual," Craig said. Sadie grabbed a dagger from under her cloak. Josh thought this was it, he was the second sacrifice. He tensed up and started jerking away but they and others in the crowd came over and held him in place.

Sadie looked at him, gave him a smile, and proceeded to cut his wrist vertically. He was bleeding pretty good now and Sadie lowered her head and began sucking ferociously on his wrist. She was done in about fifteen seconds then her head flew up and jolted backwards. She looked at Joshua with pure evil in her eyes and a big smile on her face.

Then Craig walked up and looked at Joshua and put his head down and started feeding as well. His head flew up after about thirty seconds and he stumbled away reeling from the experience. Joshua thought that the whole group would feed on him until he was dead. His wrist was in a lot of pain. Then suddenly, Brad came over and started bandaging his wrist with gauze and tape. "Don't worry Josh, is over now, your one of us."

"We just wanted a little taste of you." "Your blood's very sweet," Sadie said with a smile. Joshua grabbed his wrist after it was bandaged and the couldn't believe what had just happened.

"Do you want me," Sadie said as she took of her cloak. She was naked. Joshua had never seen a more beautiful female body. "Yes," he said with a whisper, forgetting about his wound.

She got down on all fours and turned her head and smiled at Joshua. "Take me," she said and Josh got down on his knees and took her from behind. As he was behind her she began giving Craig felatio and jerking brad off with her left hand. She took turns masturbating and giving felatio between the two. Others in the crowd were having sex too. Josh finally climaxed with a great shout.

Craig and Brad brought him to his feet and Brad said, "That's it buddy, that's as much ass you're getting for now." "Wow Josh, you felt so good inside of me," Sadie said rolled over a panting. She got up and pulled her dress back down and gave josh a kiss on the check and said, "See you tomorrow, she said sweetly." Then she ran off and joined another group of people that she obviously knew. Craig grabbed Josh by the arm and they started a slow jog towards the car.

Chapter 24

JOSH AND CRAIG were on their way towards the car but said nothing to each other. The moon was full and cast light on them as they jogged through the woods. They finally got back to the car both got in and Craig started the drive home. "My wrist really hurts." "All part of the of the greater plan, my boy," Craig said and threw Josh a joint and said, "hey lite this up." He was in no hurry on the road and he and Josh thoroughly enjoyed the joint.

When it was finished Josh through it out the window and turned and Craig who had another joint in his hand. Josh lit up. "I know you weren't expecting us to vamp out on you like that," Craig said laughing. "But those are the rites you need to do too get in the group." "You did really well, you didn't freak out too bad, I'm proud of you." "Astaroth is proud of you too, I know it." "He will come to you again soon, or maybe even Belial." "Something big is going to happen with you and the dark side." "I could feel it when I was feeding from your wrist."

They talked about some of the other demons, and spells till they got to Josh's place, just listening to the music, a little cross eyed. Josh got out of the car and looked at Craig, "You better make it to work tomorrow," Craig said half joking, half not. He reeved the car in and put in reverse. "Eight thirty tomorrow sir." He gave Josh a goodbye salute, and sped off down the hill.

Chapter 25

THINGS WERE PRETTY status quo after that. Josh went to a few other Sabbats with the folks from the office and he got to know a few other people, a few of them powerful businessmen, and influential politicians as well. He also has sex with a few women from them, but it was just sex, his heart was still with Jade. The coven was into heavy, evil, chaos, and destruction. Josh new this because they all told him quite often.

But he wasn't brainwashed like them, he really wasn't into those things, but he had to fake it. His soul was with Jade. Josh still believed the demons couldn't really have his soul because it still belonged to her. He had everything the demons promised, wealth, power, prestige and women, but he was not close to being satisfied because of her absence in his life.

He wondered when the dirty deeds would be commanded to him, it had been a couple of months with no contact. Josh found it strange but he never tried to contact them either. Josh went to work religiously and Craig always said something nice to him to show that he appreciated him. Josh new he was doing a good job. It came quickly to him.

Chapter 26

I T WAS FRIDAY, about one thirty pm, and Joshua was working
away. Friday's were awesome, everyone quit work at three, then
Craig would roll out the drink cart he had in his office and they
would party like it's 1999. Gluttonous partying, it was great. Sadie
called and he picked up, "hello you beautiful man, when we're going out
again." "Let me know when your free, and I'm up for it," Josh replied.

"Craig wants to see you in his office." "OK then," Josh said in a
puzzled voice. This was a strange request. He had been in Craig's office
all of two times since he started working. He often wondered what
Craig did in there but really he didn't want to know. Josh got up and
headed to the office quickly.

He got up to the door knocked, poked his head in "Hey, did you
want to see me boss." "Come in, come in, Josh," he said in an anxious
voice. Josh walked in to the dim office. "Have a seat," Craig said.
"Somethings happened."

"Jennings Worldwide Distibution won the bid from us, that huge
contract from those exporters from Belgium." "I'm real pissed Josh, that
guy from JWD what's his name." "Dick Jennings," Josh replied. "Dick,
Rich, whatever the fuck his name is, this guy's been a huge pain in my
ass for far too long." "Josh I need you to fix this for me." "I don't only
want the contract, I want company too, and his wife to sodomize." "So
Josh do what you need to do." "Use your influence with our demonic
friends, I want this guy destroyed." You got it Craig, I'll fix this up for
you," Josh said confidently.

"Priority One," Craig said, "I'd start working on this this weekend."
"I actually have a decent relationship with Dick," Josh started, "we run

in the same circles some times." "I drink with him a lot of times at the Boat club down on the south side of the bay." "I'll take a trip down to see him on Sunday." "I'll set it up with him right now."

"I want this fucking dealt with by mid next week Josh, before the contract is signed." "No problem sir," Josh said with a smile.

"Fuck this," Craig started, "I'm bringing the drinks cart out early today." "Come let's drink and be merry Josh, before your greatest task for me." "Yeah Craig I'm on it, I'm just going to go call Dick right now to set something up and then I'll be out to mingle."

"Hurry back Josh, let's get shitty drunk this evening." "Yes sir," he said with a laugh and walked away. In his office he poured himself a nice half class of Laguvulin with a little ice and water, lit a big joint and got on the speaker phone.

Craig didn't know it but Dick was one of them. Dick was from another Coven Josh visited time to time. Josh figured it was always good to have friends that your other friends don't know about. Josh dialed. It rang and Dick picked up. "Hello, could I please speak with Mr. Richard Jennings," Josh said. "Speaking," dick shouted back. "Hey Dick, It's Josh." "Have you meet any cock suckers lately Dick," Josh said laughing. "You see what I did Dick, Dick.....cocksucker, Ha ha." "Yeah, you Josh, and you're the biggest cocksucker of them all." "Not nice Dick," Josh replied. "What the fuck do you want Josh."

"I have to talk to you about something." "So talk," Dick said. "Come on Richard," Josh said, "you know I can't give such details over the phone." "Our phones are more bugged than Michael Mancuso." "Uncle Sam needs to know about big business dealings, it's making hordes of cash off the top earners before anyone else knows."

"I know your listening in you fuck heads, Josh yelled in the phone at the phantom IRS agents." "Why don't you all go and bugger your mothers," Josh said with an evil voice. Josh had always thought that suggesting incestuous relations with one's mother was the ultimate insult.

"So what are you suggesting," Dick said. "A tete a tete," Josh said. "Where." "Our favorite hangout." "I thought we could suck back a few drinks and talk Dick." "Oh wait Richard, I made another funny, Suck....Dick," he said laughing. "You're a fucking idiot, you're not funny, fuck face," Dick replied, getting a pissed off.

"Whenever it is convenient for you Richard but time is of the essence, it's the deal of a lifetime for both of us." "How about ten Sunday night." "Then it's a date Dick, I will see you then, have a good night." "Fuck you shithead," Dick said uninterested. "Oh and Richard, don't go and trip on your massive penis tonight and hurt yourself," Josh said laughing. "Eat my shit you fucking retard."

"What are you doing right now," Dick continued. "Smoking some green caterpillar and drinking a Laguvulin." "I'll bring you some weed Sunday," Josh said. "Have a wonderful evening Richard." "Yeah whatever," Dick cut him off and hung up.

The trap was set. Joshua didn't like fucking one of his own kind but anything to do the masters bidding. Josh thought I bet the Astaroth would be happy with him for fucking Dick over, it would be acting within his evil creed.

ZACHARIAH LEHMANN

Chapter 27

JOSH WENT OUT to join the party. Craig was already looking hammered and was head butting the other employees in the chest. Josh saw Sadie a little later and made eye contact from across the room. She seemed a little intoxicated herself. She motioned with her fist and the tongue, pushing out the side of her cheek, and he knew she wanted to give him felacio. Josh was in agreement and he nodded to her and pointed to his office. She always gave the greatest head, and Josh new after that he would fuck her violently from behind as he held her face down against the top of the desk. That's just the way she rolled. They both loved it. They both started towards Josh's office.

He woke up the next day at four pm and his head was killing. He grabbed is forehead and collapsed back to his sleeping position. Sadie had just woke up and stumbled out of bed and was headed to the living room. She sat and snorted a really big line off the coffee table. She immediately turned around with a big smile on her face and asked Josh, "What's on for today."

Josh suddenly remembered, "Oh shit, I got to do that thing for Craig." "What thing," she said. "Remember that phone call for me from Craig yesterday, well I got to do something for him." "You'll see what it's all about next week, it's a business thing," he said. "We should definitely hang out next weekend though," he said not wanting to offend her. "Sure," she said not distressed, I have to go out to see my sister anyways," she said.

"Thank you for the fucking of a life time again," she said with a little giggle. "I think you've gotten bigger since you started fucking me."

Sadie slowly got dressed and drank some of Josh's Strongbow. "Ok see you Monday hun," she said as she was finally ready.

She had taken her sweet time, it was now six. Josh waved bye as she left, then collapsed his head into his hands again reeling from the pain in his head. He was hearing that intense shock waves coming from the huge black eyes from the Primantis in his hellfire vision.

Joshua needed to talk with Belial before he met Dick Sunday night. He had a little request for him. But he didn't know how to contact Belial directly, so he thought he was going to have to summon Astaroth to get to him. He needed a plan, a plan with the most devious intensions.

He was heading into the drug store to get something for his head and this little blonde boy walked up and tugged his jacket. With the sweetest voice but a stern look and said, "you can meet Belial down where the Sabbats are in the woods." "There's a well at the northeast corner of the field, you'll see it." "The witching hour, three am sharp," then the boy took off running.

"That was definitely strange," Josh thought, "the kid had short pants on and a little suit jacket," he thought perplexed, as he walked into the drugstore. Josh went home and had a few Strongbow's. He set his alarm for one thirty and then drifted away in his bed.

Chapter 28

H E WOKE UP to the alarm blaring. He jumped in the shower to wake himself up. He got out the to the firebird about 30 minutes later. He lit up a joint and took off towards the woods. It was very and there was just a few clouds in the sky. The moon was huge and bright.

He was nervous about meeting Belial again, to say the least. He made it down to the woods, cut through some trees to and to a clearing. It was cold with the wind coming in from the bay. It was a damp, bone chilling cold. He started searching around with his flashlight. He saw something it the corner of the field and he started towards it. Josh got closer it was definitely the well, he had never noticed it before.

He looked at his watch. two fifty five am. He moved closer to it. It was very old and sinister looking, with stone blocks that were covered in black ooze emanating from the well hole. The night was completely silent as he moved in a little closer. He then started to hear very faint whisperings coming from the hole. He got closer and closer. He could now see that the well was full to the brim with this black ooze, and it was overflowing. The stench was unbearable.

Josh started to cough from it and bent down to take a deep breath. He then could make out what the whispers where saying. "he's coming, he's coming, Belial coming, Beware, Beware." He saw a few flies coming out of the ooze as he backed away a little.

Then that second, "BANG," an explosion came from the well. Josh flew back, his ass hit the ground first about ten feet away then the back of his head came slamming down on the hard ground. About thirty seconds later his head popped up and he shook it quickly. His vision was blurred but he saw he was covered in the black ooze.

He looked up and saw the horse's feet galloping, Belial's chariot behind it and his long locks of hair flowing behind him even though he seemed thousands of miles up in the sky. The moon had now turned blood red as Belial's chariot past by it which projected his image of him on his chariot into the night sky, defying the laws of physics. The image of his chariot and the horses ferociously galloping, as they past the moon, casting an ominous shadow on the moon's face. Josh stumbled to his feet and wiped the goo shit off his face. He heard the horses galloping from what seemed like thousands of miles away.

"Fucking Belial, such a fucking Pre Madonna with his entrances, he's like a musician for Christ's sakes," Josh said out loud, not thinking. Then a great fear came over him as he realized that Belial could hear every thought and word he had. He saw fog and a reddish gold light behind it at ground level. Josh new something really bad was coming.

He heard the sound of a feight train's horn that was continuous and deafening. Just then Josh saw a horse's head appear from out the front of the fog and, as if in slow motion, Belial passed him on his chariot and gave him the biggest backhand. He had a piece of steel he was wearing as armor on his forearm and had a jagged edge sticking out of it about five inches long.

When the back of his arm hit Josh's head it produced a giant gash in his forehead. He again flew back this time about 12 feet and landed the same way. He laid there a little longer this time. He stumbled again to his feet and screamed, "fuck." The blood was running heavily into his eye and as he began to wipe it out with his shirt. Then Belial descended again from the fog without his chariot, and the fog lifted. The moon was now shining its bright red glare down on them. It was like a heat lamp.

Chapter 29

BELIAL HAD LANDED and was about 25 feet from Josh, with his beautiful gold armor and still flowing black locks, and huge black eyes. He had a scary look on his face that was beyond demonic. He then began to walk quickly toward him. His head was down and he was levitating towards him. Then his head raised, "I told you Josh." Belial landed in front of him and paused again.

He then grabbed Josh by the back of his head and took off his cod piece with the other and said "open wide." His face was right in front of Belial hugeness as his head was violently pulled in to perform felacio. Josh was hacking up spit everywhere. This lasted for about three minutes then Belial pulled out and walked away a bit. Josh fell to the ground mouth still open, saliva sputtering from his mouth as he hit the ground. He was down. His head was to the side as he started vomiting.

After a few minutes he pushed himself up from the ground. His head was still bleeding from the gouge and his mouth seemed painfully stretched. He looked up and saw Belial silently levitating towards him all of the sudden and stopped for a moment.

"I'm having a light schedule after we're finished here Josh, I think when I'm done with you, I'm going to go and visit Jade." "I know where she is you see, she's in here with us." "Yeah she's a beautiful young lady." "I've thought about buggering her myself, I think that might be coming up in the very near future." "You wouldn't mind would you Josh, me ravaging your fucking girl six days from Sunday." "I'll do it as a goodbye present from you," Belial said calmly and without expression.

He knew more violence was ahead for him, and was sick at the thought of him hurting Jade. "Not tonight Josh," Belial said. "I've thought of some new plans for the rest of the evening." "Before I go and visit your beloved, I think I'll stop by your mother's grave site." "I'll have her dug up and make you sodomize her corpse while Astaroth, Azazel and I'll piss and shit all over you two." "How'd that be, eh Josh," Belial said sternly. "Then I'll skull fuck her hollow eye cavities while the other two continued shitting on her rotting flesh and bone." "I paint a pretty picture, eh Josh."

Belial then levitated right above him and came down with a mighty blow with his fist to Josh's face. He was wearing armor on his hand as well and it was like getting hit with brass knuckles with maximum force. But added to this the fists, had barb wire with huge blades sticking out of them. Belial came down with two more furious blows. With blurred vision, Josh saw Belial walking away, he turned his head and spit. Then his head feel back unconscious.

Chapter 30

JOSHUA WOKE ABOUT ten minutes later, mostly from the cold. He could barely see and he had cuts and lacerations covering his body. He couldn't talk, he tried but it felt like his lips were falling apart. He looked and could barely see Belial's chariot, with him looking into the coach about thirty feet away. He could not hear external environmental sounds, he was deaf. All of the sudden Belial's voice entered his head "wake up boy," and he grabbed two things out of the carriage, and he turned to face Josh. He slowly began to walk closer.

"I warned you once before Joshua and you didn't listen, you must always listen to what I say." "The next time I get angry with you, you won't wake up from it." And straight down there for the worst possible existence, you'll be cast in with the sodomites."

"If you think that I am a Pre Madonna and are unimpressed with my entrances, fucking keep it well to yourself, don't let your brain think that." "Show me some God damned respect." "I have the power over if you live or die and the type of existence you will have when you leave this shitty worthless planet."

Belial started to talk to him in a normal voice, "See Josh, it's all about energy." "When you filthy people die, you're not physically here anymore, but in a sense you are." "Your energy continually exists to the point where you can move between astral planes, other dimensions, and other parts of the universe."

"You can come back to this world through portals and vortexes." "You can do this for a certain period of time, but you always end up in either one of two places." "Most don't get to this point, they stay in this world clinging to some regret or past love." "Some stay to try and stop other's from passing over." "Others, the really evil ones, stay for revenge." "Those souls are my favorite," Belial said with a smile.

"How ignorant and self centered you fucking people are astounds me, but you really don't know any better." "You exploit your fellow species to the point of extinction." "You've gotten to the point of destroying your own environment so that it is uninhabitable for even you, let alone your children." "Mankind strives to be autonomous, to be a god above his fellow man." "Survival of the fittest Joshy, Darwin's one of us you know."

"You can be the biggest and the stongest gaining access to two things, power and wealth." "I find this character flaw in human nature very attractive, but it is that of our own, so it's not a flaw at all." "Mankind will do anything for their gold idle so to speak, all along pretending they belong to some religious faith." "Something that can make them think they're not that bad after all." "You people don't realize that your gods don't talk to you because they know that man is evil and beyond redemption." "Striving to be autonomous is the greatest sin Joshua," Belial said with another evil smile.

"Man does everything to be above and autonomous from his fellow man." "They want the others to be subservient to them and are most weary of their closest competitors." "Just like lion clans, they strive to be at the top of the food chain." "To be the Alpha male who stands about the rest and leads."

"They want to have control over as many of their peers as possible." "Getting the finest mate, to produce the finest offspring." "Whether it be their wives, friends, business associates, mankind wants total control over and the admiration from the people in his world."

"There are so many politicians that are truly deviant and do the will of Legion," Belial continued. "They sacrifice the good of their people, and slaughter them, to feebly try to keep their power and position."

"Look at Assad in Syria, he's almost killed a million of his own people." "He's bombed his own country into a wasteland, absolute hell on earth, for the main reason to keep control of his power and his personal wealth." "Absolutely no compassion or thought of his country or countrymen." "Did you know that modern day Syria was Ancient Babylon Josh?" "Babylon was not a very nice place Josh." "It is a place your former God was not welcome." "Assad's a big player where evil is concerned, but with little power."

"But do you know who takes the cake Josh, it's Valdy Putin." "Terrorism has been around as long as religion has been here." "But this man is the entire world's true terrorist." "He personifies the concept of evil and our ideals." "And he calls himself a president."

"Even though communism has fallen, there is no democracy in Russia." "All there voting is tracked and the people know that anyone who doesn't vote for him, will be killed." "Voting doesn't matter anyways." "He kills off as his closest political rivals," Belial said with a laugh.

"He lets his people suffer from the results of the sanctions the world has put against him, all the time he takes home around thirty billion a year through shady dealings, payoffs all other types of corruption you can think of." "He actually had the balls to go and play a hockey game with a professional team and they let him score seven goals." "He has the power of ultimate fear over his people."

"He's a walking World War Three Josh." "He could wake up hung over on the wrong side of the bed one day, stinking of Muscovite and end it all at any time, because you know he's got that red button right in his bedroom." "Legion can't even predict him, but the war will happen whether the physical world ends or not." "There would be a lot of energy displaced if it did."

"He won't even suffer when he comes to us, he'll immediately become part of Legion." "It's just the matter if he takes the rest of the world with him or not." "Absolute corruption corrupts absolutely," Belial said. "You could explain it as absolute narcissism." "In essence, humanity's goal is not to worship God, but to become gods themselves."

"Murder, lust, adultery, mutilation, anal sex, and the desire to hurt people and watch their suffering." "That instinct as a child when you don't know what murder is but you have this feeling of hate inside of you that you just want to destroy the other kid." "That moment when your vision goes blurry before you are about to strike the other kid." "Those feelings are so primal."

"But these are mere symptoms of the disease which is autonomy." "Humans, first of all recognize to protect themselves, which is why there is so much reliance on the parent in early years of life, they want people to help with their evolution." "But once the human has achieved this goal of self preservation, the need for power and to dominate their fellow man and becomes a part of life's ideal." "To be recognized as the strongest and the best, to be the person everyone else wants to be becomes paramount."

"This partly came out of the feminism, and how males started losing control of major aspects of their lives." "However society and your family has shaped you to be nice and respectful of women and to others, to have religious faith, this all goes against your primal instinct." "Men cannot take women being in power positions, it's against the natural order of things."

"Just look at how pornography has evolved." "It used to be about sexual freedom and making love and having sex to feel good." "Sex isn't about procreation anymore which was intended, its s about consensual rape and sodomy." "And this is what the porn audience expect of their mates, because they think this is now normal sex." "These new ideals makes me so happy." "To inflict as much pain and degradation as possible to prove that the male is in control is what porn has evolved into." "Sex as an expression of love is gone."

"The fags and their buggering were right all along Josh," Belial said laughing. "This sex is so unnatural and wrong in God's eyes, but it so fits with the master's principals and sway popular morals and ideals in our direction." "Porn's almost a hundred billion dollar industry Josh."

"And UFC, it's just taking your outright rage and hatred out on another human being." "I thought man would evolved beyond this by now, but I'm so glad it's still all the rage."

"There's that satisfaction of beating another person down, to visualize and let the rage and hate out." "It's like a dog or cock fight, the ideal being dominating others and inflicting carnage and even death." "And UFC is main stream Josh, five year old kids are watching this stuff now."

"Evil has its most influence on society in the present more than at any other time in history." "Maybe except for the Borgouis reign of power in the middle ages." "Evil and chaos makes sense to people now, because what they have done for thousands of years isn't working." "It is so obvious but humanity cannot see it."

"The greatest trick the devil ever did was to make man believe he didn't exist Josh." "Evil has snuck up on humanity and bit them in the ass." "There is a small portion that is not ignorant to all of this, they know the actions of the Ponzi sceamers, evangelists, murderers, political, saddists, bigots, petaphiles are wrong, but they are fascinated by these people's actions and why they do what they do." "These beautifully hideous actions are relished."

"Evil's greatest weapon in influencing the masses against good is man's inherent character flaws which Legion does everything to exploit." "We are winning Josh, and you should definitely be grateful that you are on the winning side." "The war is coming soon Josh, literally, the war to end all wars."

"Communism failed because it was innately flawed because of the ideal of autonomy Josh," Belial continued. "It was no longer that everyone was contributing and everyone was on an equal level." "Sure they might have status in society, but do you think a doctor or politician wants to be making the same amount of money as a hole digger, it's a joke."

"Capitalistic tendencies are part of humanities inherent downfall." "We in the heavens were the same way." "It's incredible how we all start out with God's ideal and in his image." "We were high up in the hierarchy of angels a part of the dominions and lordships."

"We had ultimate devotion to our Lord." "We believed in him truly, blindly and where taken to a higher state of consciousness for our complete submission to him," Belial said with a snicker. "Then there was a movement that began to develop."

"It was first just whispers, then we were talking about it out in the open." "It was the idea of autonomy." "Our devotion to God began looking more and more like slavery." "A major part of this was God's fault, he was very complacent and though he did hear the rumors of this ideology, he feared no uprising." "Instead, God took these angels ability to reason and there enheightened state of consciousness away."

"This did not have the effect that he had intended." "Without the ability to reason, the rogue angels could not see that the most reasonable thing to was to be devoted and to be protected by the Almighty." "We didn't care, we wanted God's power." "In the end there was anarchy, angels fighting over this ideal." "Others in the hierarchy joined with us as well."

"The only way to win was to combine our forces and efforts toward the trinity." "But there were still many loyal to God, led by Archangel's Michael and Gabriel, and many other casts in the hierarchy." "The heavens rained blood for many days." "After a fierce battle of brother verses brother, the divinity was eventually restored." "And we the anarchists were brought before God for judgement."

"We were hoarded in one large group, and the other angels began to advance towards us we saw a hole open up in the sky below us." "There numbers were too great and they just pushed us back, with spears and swords in hand, hacking and piercing any of us that would not move back." "God watched as one by one, we fell." "We were cast down from the heavens."

"We fell for three days," Belial said. "The first one to hit the ground was Lucifer, he was our leader, then Amon, Baal and me." "The hierarchy of the new underworld was categorized by who landed first, because who landed first were the greatest influences of the uprising." "After the dust had settled so to speak, Lucifer took immediate control as ruler, and there was no resistance."

"Lucifer stressed the power of the individual deity, but without a unified force there would be no strategic gains in this new order, and that is when Legion was born." "And the rest is how you say, history." "We began to rape and plunder humanity, preaching the ideal of surviving of the fittest."

"That why we have so many on our side, we are the easy choice, the choice that produces results and that has a man take what he wants." "We gave it to you Josh and it seems you don't appreciate it none too much." "And your God does nothing, not able to deal with the fact that man has strayed so far."

"I will tell you this Josh, you will not believe me because you think I am a trickster, but the God you once worshiped is dead." "HE COULDN'T HACK IT," Belial said loudly with a laugh." "You'll know this for yourself later on down the road." "Your right," Josh said, "I don't believe you." "Answer me this," Josh started, "not too many people have actual contact and interactions with high ranking demons the way I do, do they," he asked.

"I must have something you and your master want or I'd already be dead." "Belial turned from the chariot and started walking towards him with objects in both of his hands. Josh could hear the external environment again, and Belial was out of Josh's head and started talking to him. "Yes, your right Joshua."

"For a small percentage of your population, this extensive greed and lust for power does not affect them." "You are one of these chosen by

ZACHARIAH LEHMANN

God Joshua, that power and greed don't have an effect on." "And the fact that you came to us, Legion, on your own free will was astonishing." "But there where external factors that we influenced that kind of lead you down the path towards us, such as your childhood and your family life, that nasty priest, and others things as well."

"We matched you up with the right people I guess," Belial said with a chuckle. "And when you were introduced to Satanism, the stars aligned so to speak." He walked up to Joshua and threw a mirror that was in his right hand.

Joshua saw a flask in his left. He fumbled for the mirror and looked in the mirror at his face in horror. His jaw was knocked right out of its socket. Where there were two lips they had split into four. There were major contusions in his head. He didn't know how much longer he could endure the pain.

Both eyes were puffed out and bleeding, there was just a sliver of an eye opening in his right eyes. Belial knelt down and took Josh in his arms and opened the flask that he carried with him, and started letting Joshua drink from it. Most of it spilt on his shirt because of his lips, but he got some of it in.

Joshua instantly felt that his lifeblood was coming back. He felt his injuries healing. He leaned forward away from Belial and began to stand and to wipe his face with his hands. Belial threw the mirror to him again. He looked and saw no wounds, no scares or blood. "You came to ask me about the vision of hellfire you experienced, use it on someone, true."

"Yeah, I got this issue at work," Josh said still searching his head and body for wounds. "I need to do a little convincing with the competition and I thought showing him hellfire might do the trick." "Yes, granted," Belial said, "but you might think of giving that power back to me when you're done, you can cause a lot of damage to others with it."

They started to walk towards the chariot. "And Josh, you're going to be taking some time off work, your journey of retribution so to speak," Belial said with an evil chuckle, "is about to begin."

"You'll be meeting a friend who will help you with your adventures." "I warn you not to take his physical appearance lightly, he quite high up with us." "This is just how he chooses to manifest with humans," then Belial paused, "well at first anyways." Joshua was freezing by now, the cold air from the bay was still rolling through. Belial reached into the carriage and threw Josh a jacket.

"Oh yeah Josh," Belial said. "He took his mirror again and held it behind Josh's shoulder and held another mirror up so Josh could see." Josh saw he had three large blood filled gouges on the back of his left shoulder. Belial got into the carriage and grabbed his whip. "I know you know what three stands for, it's a physical sign of your allegiance to the cause, and your mocking of all that's good," he said with a smile and then cracked the whip. The horses started galloping. The chariot hovered above the ground toward the well, slowly at first, then it shot upward, then flew quickly down the well.

Josh stood for about ten seconds and took it all in, rubbing his head. Then he turned and started back towards the car. He was feeling the back of his shoulder and felt the deep gouges and knew the wounds would never heal, or were they meant to.

The three gouges were the ultimate fuck you to God, it symbolized the mocking of the trinity. Josh was almost to his car, It was three thirty am, and he couldn't believe that everything that just happened only took a half hour. "Belial can just screw with the concept of time," he thought. He jumped in the firebird and headed for home. He had to get some sleep and then get ready to meet Dick that night.

Chapter 31

CRAIG GOT TO the office early Monday morning. He was always early. A bit of a workaholic and an alcoholic. He grabbed a water and looked out at the Bay and wondered how many cargo ships down there were there's, or how many planes in the sky were DNL's. He turned the TV on the wall to the Business News Network and the gorgeous news anchor was talking about the CP-Norfolk merger. He looked down at the few files on his desk, few yeah right, the three would probably take four days a piece.

Then breaking news came up on the screen. "Yes, we have breaking news coming through," Pam said. "We're going to go live to Greg Smith in San Francisco." Greg came on, "thanks Pam." "Yes, huge news from the city by the bay today." "DNL has acquired all shares of Jennings Worldwide Distribution in a stunning takeover." "Both companies are major players in worldwide inporting/exporting." "Both are based in San Francisco but this is just there headquarters, these guys are global competitors."

"This deal will give DNL almost complete control of the market, making them a monopoly." Craig was already standing up, and was jumping up and down and screaming, "Joshua you bastard," yelling with elation. Greg came on again, "yes Pam, and the most amazing thing is that this is a done deal." "Wow, this just came out of nowhere," Pam said. "It certainly did," Greg responded.

"The deal was consummated late last night we understand, and the papers were signed sometime early this morning." "Richard Jennings was the sole stock holder of the company." "He was an only child and took everything when his father Walter, a shipping mogul, died in

1995." "Also amazing is DNL acquired Jenning's for thirty two billion, which is much less than what Jennings worldwide was actually worth."

"Some analysts have speculated that company was valued in excess of forty five billion." "This has sent DNL stocks through the roof trading for one hundred ten dollars a share." "These shares are now very hard to come by."

"Wow," Pam said. "And what about that huge contract with HMI that was going to be signed with Jennings?" "That has already been signed on for by a representative for DNL and HMI, so they will be reaping the profits on that deal as well."

"Josh you motherfucker, you did it, you did it," Craig yelled, still jumping and pumping his fists. He tried to call Josh on his cell but it was off. He wanted to talk to someone so bad but it was only six thirty. He decided to go over and grab his muscovite and some orange juice and lots of ice. He poured a nice big drink and just enjoyed the moment with a big smile.

Chapter 32

JOSHUA WALKED UP the stairs to the DNL building at about quarter to nine drinking a bottled water. He didn't think the news was out yet, and he couldn't wait to tell Craig. He got to the elevator and slide in just in time. The doors open and Sadie was waiting for him. "Craig's called three times now, he heard about the deal, pretty much everyone knows."

"That's so awesome Joshua, go see him," she said. He walked in and Craig was at his desk sullen, he got up and walked over to Josh and gave him a huge hug, "how the fuck did you do it man, how the fuck did you do it brother," Craid asked with tears of joy. "I'd tell you but then I'd have to kill you, literally," Joshua said giving him a hug back.

Craig grabbed Josh by the back of the head and looked him in the eyes and pulled Josh in and kissed him on the lips. "I thought you were just going to get us the deal, not take over the whole fucking company!"

"Josh we're in control of our industry now, we control shipping, and flying, and whatever else we fucking do, brother." "Nothing can take us down now, we are truly blessed by our lord Satan now my blood brother." "We are fucking gods, fucking gods on earth," Craig repeated.

"Let's not take it too far now my man," Josh said jokingly. "No seriously," Craig said, "I love you Joshua, how did you do it." "I don't want to get into the particulars because of other unearthly powers that were involved, but basically I showed him what true suffering looked like, without laying a finger on him, and saw an opportunity and took it," Josh said with half smile on his face.

"Well you're a God damn genius my friend," Craig said as he flopped back down in his leather chair looking exhausted. "And I just got word from above your under leave of absence for the next month," "You become a god and now you're leaving us."

"What do you mean from above, we're on the top floor," Josh said being facetious. "Don't be a fuck head Josh, just take the vacation as well deserved and get back as soon as you can." "This is the head office of the corporation Josh started, but I've never seen any outsiders in here and you're the boss, so what the fuck." "You know Josh I'm on conference calls all day in this office, with those parties." "Those parties are quite elusive and ominous aren't they, those that your dealing with?" "Yes Josh," Craig said sternly, "just like the parties that you deal with exclusively and don't disclose to me."

"These elusive parties are making the decisions, and we follow orders just like the little worker bees that we are." "Just know that all Legion conspires toward the same goal, it just comes out through different outlets that are sometimes human and sometimes not." "But my boy never doubt," as Craig walks over to Joshua and grabbed his cheeks, "never doubt that the universal message all comes from our dark lord."

"So don't question Josh," Craig then slaps his right cheek, just listen and do." Josh pulled away, "yeah I already knew I was going away, I was told by one of my parties a few days ago, I was just wondering if you knew anything more." "Get the fuck home, get the fuck out of here," Craig said half jokingly, half not.

"Are all the I's dotted and the T's crossed with those contracts," Craig asked as Josh was leaving. "Yeah, no worries, everything's all good, the deals are signed and just needs the underwriting done, and signatures from you for any changes to be made." "Other than that it's a done deal."

"Yeah I think I can handle that," Craig replied. So Josh, now go do whatever it is you need to do, but get the fuck out of here for the thirty days." "We'll miss you and come back safe my blood brother," Craig said with a proud smile. "Have fun my friend and thanks again for this." "Anytime my brother, anytime," Josh said as he walked out the door.

ZACHARIAH LEHMANN

Chapter 33

A S JOSH WAS jogging down the stairs he was thinking, "I got the time off now, so when do I meet my new little friend, I'm guessing soon." He got to the outer doors and was on the concrete platform and started down to the stairs to the street. He looked down and saw about twenty five reporters down at street level. Also there were news crew vans just parked in the middle of the street completely blocking traffic both ways.

He started down the steps with a grimace going to face the inevitable. Josh hated people, let alone the media. On his way down he saw Michelle from the office at the bottom of the steps and the reporters had her surrounded and were all up in here face. Josh didn't know why, she was order taker from the second floor.

She looked up and saw Josh. "There you guys, there's Mr. Joshua, he's the one who got the deal done." "I'm so sorry Mr. Joshua," as the hoar ascended the steps to get to him, "It's just I don't know anything, and they wouldn't leave me alone." "It's ok," he shouted back, not blaming her at all.

The reporters got up to him, phones, recorders and news cameras all in his face. "Sir, were you the one who negotiated the deal between Jennings and DNL." "Yes, I did represent DNL in regards to that matter," Josh replied. "Mr. Joshua, can you explain how the deal came about for the biggest takeover in U.S. shipping history, and how your company came out the most advantages by far and away."

"Just lucky I guess," he said to laughter. "Listen," Josh said with a smile. "I'm not going to discuss any of the details of the negotiations." "Dick and I go back a few years." "We started talking the other night about business and what made sense for both parties." "Dick's just not fond of the business anymore and he wanted to do other things for himself and his family." "You have to respect the man for that." "We settled on a fair price," Josh said as he got laughs from the media.

One of the reporters shouted, "fair price, you swindled the man, you got Jennings for 9 billion less than market value." "How did you do that."

"You people and whoever these so called appraisers are, don't know what you think you know," Josh started, "In a takeover there's a ton of bad debt to be written off, labor that will be laid off that will save money in the future, but very costly in the short term." "Also there's the expense of getting Jennings buildings, ships, and planes up to code, and there in pretty dire straits right now," Josh replied feeding them shit.

"Also, scrapping million dollar projects that Jennings was involved in that don't fit DNL's business model." "All of these factors are involved in settling on a price," Josh explained. "You have no conception of these expenses because they are not made public."

"What about the word from Vatican City today," the female reporter asked. "The financial sector of the Catholic Church that runs its corporations and business's will no longer deal with DNL Corp., for what they refer to as deviant, unethical, and illegal business dealings and commodities trading."

"They say they have proof of the shady practices, such as shipping everything from illegal ivory to large shipments of narcotics." "They also accused DNL of being involved in illegal human trafficking and supplying dictators in Africa and the Middle East with weapons to wage war and perform acts of genocide on their own people."

"Well, well, well, isn't that scandalous," Josh said in a monotone voice. "I think that's pretty funny, Josh said." "Why is that funny Sir," they asked. "Because I'm a Catholic," Josh said as he took his wallet out, producing a business card. He got the card when he was at an AA meeting at a church, in another one of his fruitless attempts to get clean. He thought it was cool and he felt protected by it for some reason.

The card red, I am Catholic. In the event of an accident or serious illness, please call a priest. The Catholic Health Association of California. The media laughed when he read it to them. "See this proves everything, I'm a good Catholic boy just like we all are here at

DNL." "We all go to church together," Josh said sarcastically and they continued laughing."

"No, seriously I have never heard of any shady business dealings, or negotiating in bad faith, or trading violations." Josh wasn't lying, he never knew what Craig and those "parties above him," were up to. They could have been shipping Afghanistan whole gross domestic product for all he knew. All Joshua knew, because he was high up in the front office, was that were teams of associates at DNL that were in charge of falsifying contracts and documents and that the companies on the other end of these business dealings were all bribed very well, and they were sent the false proof of the transactions.

"And if the church is referring to our new acquisition, how would they know anything about it." "There was only Dick and myself in the room, unless they were looking through a peep hole in one of the paintings on the wall, I definitely saw no one else there." "I have access to any records of transactions or contents of shipping deliveries just as you the media have access to these contracts just by contacting DNL public relations." "We have nothing to hide."

Joshua started towards his car that was waiting on the street. "I'm done with this," he said in frustration as he pushed the reporters in front of his car door away. "Please show some respect and let me go home to my family," (which was also a lie, he had no family). "Wait," the female reporter said, "why do they call you Mr. Joshua here."

"I don't know," he said perplexed, I do have a last name, that's what they've called me from the beginning so I just went with it," he said with a chuckle. Josh ducked in the back seat and the driver sped off down the road.

Chapter 34

I T HAD BEEN three days since the media hoard at work. It seemed Joshua had a few days off while he was waiting for the appearance of his mystery friend. He had been trying to lay low. No one had called from work, I guess they knew not to. He had been trying hard not think of the whole satanic situation. But when your trying not to think about something, that's when you can't get it out of your head. He was still feeling guilty for screwing Dick, but then he finally thought how Dick had gotten off really easy after all.

Firstly, he was still alive and he still had his family. And he also had thirty two billion dollars to play with now. That kind of money would get you ahead in any game he wanted to play. He was just upset about taking his family business, the business his dad had built from the ground up, and for fucking him up mentally with the hellfire vision.

He couldn't get a look at Dick's face when he was experiencing it. His expression must have been the same when he had seen it. Pure and utter horror. He remembered the vision vividly as well. "So eerie," Josh thought, "especially the overpass leading to the well and the giant Primantis, that was pretty fucked up."

But he was promised that he would not end up with that fate. He also never could get Jade out of his mind, as much as he tried. He loved her now more than ever and her absence just left him more and more depressed. It was true in his demonic pact, he could pretty much have any woman he wanted. He was always getting the come hither look, while he was out in public. Some of the girls would just come up and blatantly hit on him or give him their number.

One girl even followed him into the washroom at the food court in the mall one day, dragged him into a stall, stripped and said she was ready for him and started undoing his pants. Josh pulled his pants back up and politely declined. And these were very good looking, sexy women who were smart and morally loose as well. But every time he interacted with a female he could only think of Jade, he only wanted her.

Sadie was so awesome because she never put pressure on him and they were always emotionally on the same page. She was someone he trusted to talk to and use for sex whenever he wanted. She always made herself available to him, day or night. And she would never say anything about whatever they talked about, even to Craig. He had even spoke with her about Jade, he had cried in front of her, but Sadie never judged him, she only listen and was sympathetic.

Lying low wasn't going very well as Josh had spent the past few nights at the James Joyce shooting the shit with Sergei, the Irish Russian, and they actually had some meaningful discussions. They got into a really big thing about the plight of the Chechniyans and there terrorist war on Russia. He learned a lot from Sergei last night. He wanted to go take up arms with the Chechniyans and fuck Russia up. Especially that fucking Putin, Josh kept on thinking "I'm going to get you Putin, you fucking bastard," as he got more and more drunk.

He was saying what he was thinking out loud again. Always dangerous. Especially when you're shouting so load whole bar room of people heard him talking about his plots to assassinate the President of Russia. People were looking at Josh and shaking their heads. A very good example of why not to talk politics in a bar. Another lesson Josh should have learned was how to leave a bar before you are too drunk to find your way out. "Well not tonight," Josh said aloud to himself. He thought that talking to yourself is one of the great advantages of living alone.

He had woken up earlier with one of those hangover's you can get rid unless you continue to drink heavily. He had woken up at six that night and he had been watching movies and smoking weed laced with a little PCP and drinking.

Chapter 35

IT WAS NOW about quarter to three am on the next day. He had consumed a magnum of wine, 8 tall cans of Strongbow, and had smoked four joints. Josh was feeling pretty good at that point. He headed out on the patio to smoke another one. He walked out, sighed, took a deep breath and stretched out his arms.

Now, Josh's patio looked over a large revene that was in the middle of his neighborhood. It was a beautiful night, a little cold but he was warm blooded so it didn't bother him. He looked down on the revene and wondered if there was anyone getting raped or killed down there. There were some bad people in this city and Josh knew a lot of them from his time working at the bar, and the after hour's scene.

He walked back to beside the door where the light was, and lit up. Some of the trees had grown quite tall on the hill leading up to his place. Three of them had even grown higher than the patio railing itself. He coughed a little, the weed was really laced. He looked up at the sky. He could tell it was clear because the moon was full and shining brightly.

Then he saw something moving in one of the trees that was above him. He looked and there seemed to be a small figure in the tree and it was moving. He moved in a few steps to get a closer look and all of the sudden the light beside his door shattered and exploded onto the ground, scaring the shit out of him. "What the fuck," Josh thought, there was nothing there to break the light, and it was one of those solid LED lights that was supposed to last thirty years or something.

Josh then heard something coming from the tree. It was a child's voice singing. He heard the child singing, "hush hush hush, here comes the boogeyman, don't let him come to close to you he'll catch you if he can, just pretend that you're a crocodile and you will find that boogeyman will run away a mile." He stepped in a little closer. The moon was bright and he could make out the outline of a small person sitting on one of the trees sturdy branches.

The figure was not moving except for one of its legs was swinging back and forth towards him. The outline of It's head was staring directly at him.

"Good morning Josh," the small figure said. Josh thought he was hallucinating from the PCP, and walked in a few steps further. "That's close enough," the figure said. He could see a lot better now with the lights from the road. It was that little boy with the short pants and the little suit jacket that told him where to find Belial. He looked so Arian with his platinum blond hair and his big ice blue eyes. Josh was really high and drunk, and was a really freaked out.

"Hey, I know you," Josh said slurring, "you're the little tike that told me where Belial was that day on the street." "What are you doing way up in that tree little guy, you're going to fall down and hurt yourself." The boy snickered and said, "Yes, your right Josh, I am small in stature, but remember how Belial told you that looks are deceiving." "The boy in front of you is just an image your puny brain can process."

"My true image is inconceivable to you, your heart would stop and you would die at the site of me." "There is ultimate power beyond your comprehension in this little body." "My master is also your master, Josh." "I have come to help you get your shit together and get your tasks done." "I'm here to make sure that you follow the orders from Legion that I pass on you to the tee." "My name is man, and don't fuck with me Josh, or I'll make the beating you took from Belial look like child's play," man said with his tiny little voice.

"You should have died that night Josh, but instead Belial resurrected you, I don't know how you got to consult with him, I don't know how you got past Astaroth to tell you the truth." "He wants you because your marked for salvation at the end time." "He's studying you and your kind to see if there is some kind of pattern were he can tell which of the humans will survive the apocalypse." "This far, we have only found out that about eighty percent of you are left handed which is unusual because left handed people only comprise of one in ten humans." "The marked, if you will, come from all walks of life and every continent and are every skin color and creed.

"Belial's a curious fellow, he's had a little side project going for the last ten thousand years on trying to understand the human condition and how they evolved." "I don't know why, you humans aren't worth shit." "I guess it's the fact that humans are generally very predictable, but at the same time you can act so randomly and suddenly just lose it." "Belial studies humanity's behavior and also has great influence on society's downfall as well." "He is the chief of all devils." "He is dedicated to creating wickedness and guilt in humankind."

"Belial's name in ancient texts means without worth Josh." "We are filth Josh, we are here to cause chaos and bring the down fall of mankind through the destruction of their values and ideals." "Belial and our kind are known in the heavens as the adversary, the opposed." "We are the complete opposite of everything that is innocent, pure and inherently good." "He's higher up that me Josh, and he has been apart of training me and my crafts, I guess as humans would say." "He is the leader of the Sons of Darkness, he really is the high sheriff of hell Josh except for the Amon, Baal, and my master, that is."

Josh was swaying now and had a little smile, he was pretty intoxicated at this point, and he was trying hard to take it all in. "Joshua, I'm the chief emperor of the south and responsible for its demise, Lucifer controls the North. I rule over 200 great dukes, 400 lesser dukes, and 1,000,200,000,000 ministering spirits. "Well that's a great resume little guy." "Yes … Josh" man continued. "So why don't you do something good then," Josh said.

"Start a war in the Middle East, I know a big fucking meteor and tsunami should do the trick as well, or a big fucking earthquake." "In time Joshua, in time," man said quietly. "And forget about what you did to Dick, that's child's play. "We're going to get our hands and all of our parts bloody on this one Joshua, it's going to be a bloodbath," man said in his tiny voice starting to giggle, which scared the shit out of Josh.

"Ok, this is a fun little game for us to get to know each other." "Well I know everything about you, but you don't know who I am." "I know you have done some readings in demonology Josh, so tell me, what is my Demon name from the description I gave to you from before." "I don't know, my little friend, the brain's not working to well this evening, but I will give it a valiant effort when I get straight tomorrow."

"Well get that done before we meet tomorrow," Man said with his stern little boy face. Joshua's mind drifted from the conversation. He

ZACHARIAH LEHMANN

was used to these incredibly bizarre meetings now. He looked up at man, the moon was very big and bright above him and the sky was clear, it still made man look like a shadow. He just looked up at him drunkenly and thought, "well, aren't you a nasty little shit, I'm going to come over and shake you out of that tree and spank your bare ass."

Josh was flying backwards again. He hit the wall of his house underneath the light hard. He was on his ass against the wall, "oh my fucking head, again with my fucking head." Joshua looked up and gave man a nasty glare. "OH Joshua, Man was laughing histaracally, his little legs still swinging, "that mind and mouth of yours will be the death of you."

"So sober the fuck up Josh, get some sleep, we're going to meet at the crack of noon to discuss some travel plans." "And really Josh, PCP, people did that shit twenty five years ago, do you want to end up literally retarded." "You already have a few to many vices, plus so many blows to the head isn't helping," Man said still laughing. "Try and save the few brain cells you have big guy."

"Man looked straight up at the moon and his childlike face illuminated. He pushed himself off the branch, and gave Joshua a wink while he fell into the darkness of the revene." Josh walked over and looked down, just as he figured, just trees and hill and the park below him. Josh couldn't think anymore he was so tired. He went upstairs and slipped into bed with his clothes on, still on grabbing to the back of his head.

Chapter 36

OSH WOKE THE next day and he was semi conscious for the first twenty minutes while he lied there frightened and sad that Jade was still gone. Then the brain kicked in, "Holy Shit, what time is it." He looked over and saw it was ten forty and laid back down. This all still seemed like a dream when he woke up like this, but he knew that this was his reality and it was very, very real. "Oh that little shit wants me to find out who he is," he said aloud as he flung himself out of bed.

Even though eating was not a remote possibility at this time, he made his way to the kitchen to put the kettle on. He went to sit down then remembered he had to get his demonology encyclopedia. He had read it cover to cover and knew that most of the really big boys where found from A-C.

He went through them and read the major demons accomplishments, titles and contributions to human misery. He got to the beginning of C and thought he was going to have to go through the whole book Then he saw one that he had not spent too much time on and started reading. From what he remembered of last night, those where the exact credentials man was bragging about.

Man's demon name was Caspiel. It said that all of the Dukes of Hell are stubborn and churlish, but many attend Caspiel when he appears, he read as he sipped his tea. "Sounds like a real peach", Josh thought. He looked up and it was saw it was eleven thirty five. He made his way up to the bathroom, brushed his teeth, and jumped in the shower. He got dressed in his khaki shorts, his hoody, his Birk's, and headed out to the patio for a smoke.

It was eleven forty nine, so he still had time to enjoy his joint. He lit up and peaked over the edge, half expecting man to be down there early. He started pacing for a bit realizing that he must control his thoughts about the demons in their presence, or he didn't fucking know what they'd do to him. Plus he would need to think critically, because Man would definitely want his input.

Chapter 37

JOSH LOOKED UP through the tree at the bright sun, and then he saw man crawl through the light and haze, and down the tree. He then paused for a minute and stood and balanced himself on one of the branches. Then he jumped over onto the patio and fell on his feet with his knees buckling like a gymnast. He then popped up and with a smirk on his face dusted himself off. "Wow Josh, you're looking way more presentable than last night." "But Josh really, you couldn't have been a little more dressy, look what I'm wearing," as he looked down at his little suit with a smile.

"Caspiel," Josh said. Josh looked him in the face and said, "your demon name is Caspiel." "Very Good Joshua, I am impressed that you remember anything from last night you fucking lush, but I still want you to call me man." "It kind of represents to me what humanity should strive to be, as we go to rape, pillage, and murder." "I am the image of a child, innocent, pure, and vulnerable." "Are you going to save me Josh," man asked with a little laugh.

"Come now Josh, were going to take a walk so you can clear your head and we can have a discussion." Josh followed man up the stairs beside the house and down the driveway, where he so wanted to jump in the firebird and get the fuck out of there, but he knew that wasn't a possibility. "Where are we going," Josh asked. "The park at the bottom of the hill."

"Tell me something Joshua, what did you really want when you sold your soul." "I know you said what basically everyone else says, that's human nature." "I didn't want to be lonely anymore, I wanted to be with Jade forever and I thought this was the way," Josh said honestly.

"And you wanted to know that if she did leave, which thinking of was so painful for you, that you would always have someone else that would be provided." "I also wanted people everywhere to recognized me and be in admiration and awe of me, thinking I was such a great person."

"Wow, and you just wanted this even though you knew that you had contributed nothing to society to warrant such admiration." "Yeah, pretty much that was the idea," Josh responded. "Umm, where's Jade and how is she," Josh said sadly and almost to himself. "I'm not sure where she is Josh, I'm assuming she's fine," man responded. "There were no big plans for her that I heard of." "What I can guarantee you Josh is that you WILL see her again, there's no question of that." Josh felt so happy.

They entered the park and they looked around. There we're a few couples with kids but it was mostly single mothers who came to socialize and talk while there kids played together. And then there was those couple of guys in track pants and the hats and sunglasses. "If there was a uniform for a petephile, that would be it," Josh thought. "This priest is in San Diego, the one that raped you," Man asked.

"That's what Belial told me, when I signed my soul over." A mother came walking by and said, "Oh well, isn't that boy darling," "those big eyes are ice blue." "I've only seen that once before, and that outfit." Man was looking up at her unimpressed. "Oh thank you so much," Josh said while dragging Man along. "He's my precious little boy, aren't you." Josh continued. Man gave Josh the dirtiest look.

"I want to leave tonight." "I want to get settled and let you sleep." "It's Sunday tomorrow and I want to be there for when he participates in mass at eight thirty." "What time do you want to leave," Josh asked. A different women came running at them, "oh my God, where did you get that outfit for your boy." Man hissed at her and Josh quickly grabbed him by the scruff of the collar, "don't touch me you nasty hag, or I'll rip your God damn tits off," he said.

That stopped her in her tracks. "Oh my, what did your boy say to me." "Sorry about that, he's been sick and a little anxious lately." Josh then changed the subject. "Yeah, you know where we got it, we were visiting our relatives in England, and I actually picked them up at a thrift shop in Liverpool." Josh meshed Man's little hat and hair up. Man looked up and gave Josh the stink eye, as Josh pulled him along. "Have a good day," Josh shouted back at her.

"This is ridiculous, I gotta get the fuck out of here," man said. "Do you know how many nice women I could pick up with you under different circumstances," Josh laughed down at man, and then he thought of Jade again and that shut him up. "Focus Josh," was Man's only reply. "What time tonight," Josh repeated. "Be ready for three thirty."

"We'll do the priest quickly, because I want to get to L.A. to start on the next guy." "There a very short time line for this Josh," man continued. There was a cab parked on the street at a break in the fence. "Let's head toward the cab, I have to go deal with this thing downtown, be in the car waiting at three thirty," man commanded. Man opened the door and crawled into the backseat, "fifty seventh and twentieth," he said in his tiny voice, the cabby looked back and did a double take.

The cabbie looked up at Josh. "No, No, No, I won't be responsible for this child." Josh reached in his back pocket and gave the cabbie forty dollars. "Hey listen, have you ever seen on TV," Josh started, "those little people that just stay little and they look like there still like five years old." "Yeah," the cabbie said scared, "I have seen that, it's pretty freaky."

"Yeah, well he's sixty four years old," Josh said looking down at Man. "Look at the way he's dressed." Man was innocently smiling at the cabbie. "And If you don't take him down there he's going to sue your ass for discrimination." "Yeah my friend, I don't need no trouble, let's go little guy," the cabby said as Josh closed the door and flagged his own cab to take him back up the hill to his place.

Chapter 38

JOSH WAS WAITING in the car all packed at three thirty. Man walked out from the side of the house. He got in and said "let's get er done." They made it to the Hilton in San Diego at about quarter to one. Josh had a couple ciders that he brought and another joint. Then he passed out on the bed exhausted from the trip and fell asleep, while man sat in a chair staring out the window listening to Bach on his I pod.

They pulled into the church parking lot at about 8 am. The church was nice. It wasn't tradition, it was high and shaped like a semi circle with a large stain glass steple at the back center. They walked in and the ground floor was almost three quarters full. "Let's go up to the balcony," man said while pulling Josh by the hand. The balcony was pretty much empty except for an elderly couple and a family of four, which were both sitting in the back. Josh and man sat in the first row overlooking the floor. "We can talk better up here."

The service started and everyone was standing and made the sign of the cross, all except man, who was wincing. There was a young priest leading the mass, and Masterson was seated in a big chair at the right side of the Alter, by the Alter boys. He looked a lot shorter than what Josh had remembered, that's probable because Josh's last memory of him was when he was 7.

He was thin from disease and old age, and looked feeble and pathetic. It made Josh feel good. His duties had deminished with his age and mental condition, to simply serving communion. He was more of a figure head now. They all sat.

"Josh I wanted to remind you why we are killing these people, because they are trying to repent with their actions now, the evil they unleashed in the past." "They don't know they are already ours, there is no repentance for what they did to you and many others," man said whispering. "We are going to take them before the Nazarene has a change of mind and chooses redemption for them, which he does from time to time."

"So here's the plan, I've got the intel from the boys downstairs." "They gave me Masterson's private number." "He lives in the rectory two doors down from the church." "He finishes drinking about 11 pm." "He's got Korsakoff's disease so his mind is demented." "You will call him from the front of the church at about 10pm while he has some wits about him."

"You'll call and tell him that you have just committed murder, and that you must repent so that you can save your soul." "He'll come over and offer to perform confession for you, and try to get you to turn yourself in." "It's in the confessional that you will confront him with your anger and rage." "Then you will bring him alive up to the roof, using that staircase," as he nodded to the stairs across the building, "where I will meet you."

The young priest suddenly looked up. He looked over and man and the priest's eyes met. Man had an evil little smile on his face while he stared at the Priest. The priest had continued his Eulogy while still locked with man's eyes, but was now speaking in Latin.

He began to speak louder and louder. He finally broke man's glance and began to shake and stumbled to the floor for a quick second, and then recovered. "This is the word of God," the Priest said sullenly from behind the Alter. "Praise be to Lord Jesus Christ," the congregation returned loudly and in unison.

"I have to warn you though Josh," man continued, "I like to make my offerings to the master quite creative, especially where priests are involved, so you're in for a bit of a treat."

The mass had continued and it was almost time to give out communion signifying the end of the service. People began to line up to receive communion. "What about getting caught," Josh started, "what about DNA." You don't have to worry about that. How can I explain this, man said, Belial has granted you shapeshifting DNA."

"The evidence they find at the scene will be that of someone of Belial and my choosing." "So who is this murder going be pinned on," Josh asked. "I didn't know until now but it's going to be that fucking smug priest down there," man said. "I'll teach him to get self righteous with me."

Communion was now done and the priest was reading church announcement. After he said, "The mass has ended let us go in peace." The congregation replied. "We go in piece to love and serve the Lord." The people on the alter including the Alter boys(one holding the cross) the priest, Masterson, someone who seemed to be a deacon, and a women holding the bible above her head. They started walking down the center isle to the back of the church, as the congregation sang hymns praising God. Man and Joshua started down the stairs. At the bottom of the stirs the Priest was shaking hand and talking to the parishioners.

They were almost out the door and the priest left his conversation and came over to them. "Hello," he said, "I have never seen you two here before, where is this child from." "I have just come from buggering your whore of a mother," man said under his breath. The priest looked down on him. Josh started "we're just here from out east visiting some family." "Wow the west coast is so beautiful." "We're leaving to go back home tomorrow."

"I'm glad to hear that," the priest started, "And if you ever do come back for a visit, never bring that child into this Parrish again," he said with a stern look, and went back over to saying goodbye to the people. "We'll you made quite an impression," Josh said laughing as they descended the stairs, I didn't think we were in there that long.

"Don't you worry," man said in a confident voice, "I'll get that fucking priest and his little dog too," and he and Josh cracked up with the Wizard of Oz reference. They both jumped in the car, "where to now my little friend." "We have to go shopping." "Where shall we shop." "I need a hardware store first, we got to pick up the stuff for tonight." "Wow, a hardware store, we're in for an enjoyable evening," Josh said sarcastically. "Focus Josh," was man's only reply. Josh found a hardware store on the GPS and they were off.

They got to the store, and it was huge inside, Josh wondered how they were going to find anything he wanted. "Don't worry Josh," man said, "I know where everything is." So Josh just followed the man, pushing a huge cart that was meant for carrying lumber in it. The first item was about fifty feet over rope. Man grabbed the rope and said, "see, it's got to be the stretchy kind," as he pulled on the rope. "Alright," Josh responded. Next was a saw. "It's got to be the smallest but sharpest one they have." "And electrical tape, and a metal cutter."

"Ask that guy who works here, he's over there," Man commanded and pointed. Josh went over to talk to the guy and he was able to pick something out pretty quick. "This is the smallest and the sharpest," he told man as he threw it in the cart. Next they went to get some crazy glue, metal cutter, and tape for God knows why. "That it, we're done." "Honestly Josh, I don't know why you picked such a big cart, we were only here to pick up a few things," as he walked ahead, Josh scowling at him." "I see that face," man said while not even looking back at Josh's scowl.

Then Josh put a big smile on his face and remembered not to think bad thoughts. They stopped at a thrift shop and picked up an old tracksuit for Josh to wear so he wouldn't get his real clothes bloody. Then they made their way back to the hotel.

Chapter 39

JOSH WAS SMOKING weed and drinking heavily until when eventually Man scolded him, saying that he needed to keep his wits about him. Man was listening to his I pod, Josh could hear the classical music coming out of it, he had no idea who the composer was. Josh finally laid down in bed and curled up for a quick nap.

He was doing anything to keep out of his head what might be coming up tonight. He drifted off pretty quickly into a blackout. The next thing he heard was "wake up Josh," man was saying from the bathroom. Josh looked over and man was up on the bathroom sink. He was watching himself in the mirror, throwing fake punches and dancing around the bathroom countertop like he was getting ready for a boxing match. He almost fell a few times. Then he did a summer salt in the air while jumping down and said, "it's time to get ready Josh, it's nine fifteen."

Josh took about three Ativan and went in the washroom to get ready, while man sat in his chair and stared off into space listening to his music. Josh took a quick shower, grabbed change of cloths, another two Ativan's, and the baby wipes he bought to get rid of the blood on his skin. He had no Idea of what he was walking into and he had been very anxious, but never asked man about what was going to happen, because he knew that he wouldn't tell him.

It was nine thirty and they headed over to the church. They parked down the street from the church in a small convenient store parking lot. The store was already closed. It was really quiet, Josh got what they brought out of the trunk and they started heading up the hill. They got into the church parking lot and they were beside the wall of the church and Josh put the stuff down. "Ok Josh, showtime." "I'll meet you on the roof with the priest." "And mind the time Josh, we don't have all night."

"Say your peace, and then destroy him," man said with no expression. "How are you going to get that stuff to the roof," Josh asked. Man threw the rope over his neck to the opposite shoulder, put the crazy glue and metal cutter in his pockets, grabbed the small saw and put it blade first into his mouth and bit down on the blade so it wouldn't cut him. He then proceeded to start to crawl up the church wall like Spiderman.

He moved horizontally, then straight up to the highest level of the roof, then flung himself upwards and landed on the rooftop out of Josh's sight. Josh was stunned, but not surprised and proceeded with the plan. Josh had Masterson's number programmed so he just hit the button and the phone was ringing. "Hello," Masterson answered sounding a little out of it. "Oh father," Josh started, "I can't believe what I've done, God forgive me," he shouted away from the phone and started wailing.

"Now son, calm down," Masterson replied. "I can't father, I can't, I can't believe it, I killed my wife father, I killed her, she's dead," and Josh started sobbing. "I had nowhere to go father, I was downtown at the shelter cleaning myself up and going crazy, pacing and sobbing." "Then one of the guys I knew down there came up to me and gave me your number." "He was like an angel and all he said was, call Father Masterson up at St. John's, and that he you were the only one who would care enough about a stranger to help me." "And now I'm up here father, and I need confession because I believe this is the only way to save my soul," Josh said still sobbing.

"You're at the church now," Masterson asked. "Yes Father, and I believe if your not able to help me, I will take my own life and lose my soul forever." "Please help me Father," he said with complete dispair in his voice. "Yes son, I will help you." "I'll come down as soon as I can, just give me about ten minutes to get ready." "In the meantime, just sit on the church steps, take some deep breaths and try to calm down the best you can, ok," and Masterson hung up.

Josh put the phone away. He had the shitty track suit on and messed his hair up so he looked like he had just come from the shelter. He got his flask of vodka out of his pocket and started swilling and sat down on the steps like Masterson had instructed. He continued drinking, then about fifteen minutes later he saw Masterson doing a slow jog down the

ZACHARIAH LEHMANN

road towards the church. He took a few more drinks and put the flask away as Masterson made his way up the stairs.

Josh was seeing him up close now, and the hatred and rage started festering inside of him. He was still sobbing with the crocodile tears looking very pitiful. Josh jumped up to greet Masterson and grabbed him by both hands and said, "thanks for coming father." Masterson looked frightened and intimidated by Josh's size. "Yes, let's go inside," he said. The priest unlocked the front doors of the church and they went in. Josh could smell the whiskey coming off of him. Masterson was leading and they were headed to the side of the church where the confessionals were.

"I have to tell you my son, I will help you, confession is vital for the soul in these instances." "But I will tell you that if you do not turn yourself in after this, then God and I will both turn our backs on you." "I understand Father, and I am willing to do that."

Masterson turned to him and grabbed him by the hands and said as they reached the confessional, "that is the most important thing and I am proud of you for taking responsibility for this," he said with slurred words. Masterson was shitfaced. "But father, I have to talk with you about something else before I make the confession." "What can be more important than this," Masterson asked and fell backward a bit.

"Well it's a story from my past that you need to know first," as the priest motioned for him to go through the velvet drapes and into the confessional. They both sat and Josh started, "Bless me father for I have sinned, it has been sixteen years since my last confession." "Yes, I think this story will help explain some of my actions, and it's not too long." "Go ahead," Masterson said.

Josh paused for a minute then started, "when I was a boy, about 7 years old I guess, I was pretty sheltered from sin and wickedness from where I lived and by my family, especially my mother, and I loved her a great deal." "I was an Alter boy as well, and it made me feel special at the time, it made me good that I was part of the church and the mass." "The Priest taught me a lot in the first three months about how to act and behave."

"I almost had love for the priest like I had for my own family." "One day after mass, I was helping take down the Alter." "This priest came out from the back grabbed me by the hand and took led me to a storage room in the basement of the church." "I was so scared because I thought I was in trouble, but I couldn't think of what for."

"When we got in there this priest that I had grown to love, he was drinking whiskey and stumbling around, talking about things I didn't understand, adult things." "Do you know what happened next father," Joshua asked looking through the screen at Masterson, who was staring straight forward in silence. "That priest overtook me in that downstairs room and he raped me so violently that I bleed from my anus for three straight days." "He then discarded me in the churches back yard, left me to die."

Josh had been talking monotone up until that point but a lot of emotion was now coming threw in his voice. Masterson started sobbing. "And you know father, It wasn't the violent act and the betrayal of the priest that was worst about the whole thing," Josh said as Masterson continued to weep while Josh was talking. "It was that I basically didn't have parents anymore, because they wouldn't believe that a priest could have done that to me," Josh said raising his voice. "I lost my mother to drugs and my father disowned me." "Do you understand the guilt and loneliness that I felt growing up, it was almost unbearable," Josh asked with his voice starting to shake.

Masterson started speaking while he was whimpering. "I have flashbacks and horrible nightmares of what I did to you boys." "My brain doesn't work to well anymore," Masterson said crying, "it was all the booze." "I would black out so much back then." "I get physically ill every time I get a vision," Masterson said." I do feel a lot of guilt, but it is the absolute shame that haunts me most."

"I wanted to quit drinking for this to stop happening, but I couldn't because the booze was the only way for me to forget my constant torture." "Please don't hurt me," Masterson begged through the screen, "I have the disabled and the elderly I take care of and who wouldn't survive without me."

We'll they'll have to find someone else, Josh said coldly. "You know the murder I spoke of earlier Father." "Yes, Masterson said weeping. "Well I'm confession to your murder." "You're my first kill Father," Josh said in a monotone voice. "The reaper has come for you my old friend," he said with a smile.

Josh's fist smashed through flimsy screen and struck Masterson right between the eyes. Josh ran over to the priest's side and gave him

ZACHARIAH LEHMANN

two more shots to the head and a knee to the chest. Masterson was sitting on the floor of the confessional all crumpled up. He was still sobbing weakly so he was still conscious. Josh grabbed him and dragged him out of the confessional, then picked him up and threw him over his shoulder. Masterson weighed next to nothing, and Josh made his way over to the stairwell that led to the roof.

As he walked up the latter, the priest just keep repeating, "fuck your ass, fuck your ass," while he was draped over Josh's shoulder, which made Josh wonder what he was talking about. Did he want to fuck Josh in the ass again, or was he saying it like saying "screw you." He got to the roof, took a few steps and then Josh dropped him and walked over to the edge of the roof.

Chapter 40

THE FIRST THINK he noticed he couldn't hear any external audio again. Then he looked up at the moon and it was in an eclipse in front of the sun. But it couldn't be the earth's sun because it was night. And the ring around the black moon was blood red. He looked at the houses in front of him and down the street. There was no lights on in any of the houses, there were no people or cars.

The barometer had dropped like there was a tornado coming. Suddenly, an enormously loud squeal. He turned and looked down the street where the noise came from. There down the road was Azazel underneath a bus stop. "If you want to see her again, don't fucking give up on this," Azazel said and the voice rang through his head again. He dropped to his knees and tried to cover his ears but the words would not stop ringing in his head.

Suddenly it stopped and he heard man's voice from behind him, "are you ready for this Josh." He turned around and there was man standing beside Masterson, who was lying face up on the roof. His chest was moving and he was moaning so he was still alive. The things he had brought up along were with man, along with two leather wipes. "Where the fuck did you get the wipes," Josh asked. "I bought them up when you were inside with the cunt," Man answered, "I didn't want to ruin the surprise." Josh walked over looking at the old man. Man picked up a whip and tossed it to Josh, then picked up his own.

Man turned around for about ten seconds, then turned and came down with a thunderous slash on Masterson. It sounded like Masterson was trying to scream but he didn't have the life left in him. Man stared at Josh with an evil look on his face and then came down on him with another slash. Masterson's body jumped with the force of the blow and he was now crying.

"Go ahead Josh, do it," man said with a smile. "Do you remember what this fuck did to you." Josh felt the hatred grow inside. "Do remember the pain of him inside you." Josh started breathing heavy. He came down with a big lash on Masterson himself. It felt really good for him. "Good Josh, again." Josh slashed again and started getting a rhythm going with his wiping.

He couldn't hear Masterson anymore, just man's voice. "Remember your happy innocent life before he did this, and now think of the misery and anguish you went through after this fuck did had his way with you." Josh's slashes were speeding up and he was raining down thunder on Masterson. Man joined in the whipping. He would whip when Josh reeled back so they weren't in unison. It was one slash after the other, constant torture for Masterson, if he could still fee it.

The both of them rained down vicious blows on him for about five minutes, then Josh broke away and dropped the whip, gasping for air. He bent over and was hyperventilating for another two minutes and then realized that it was over. "Oh it's not over, Joshua," man said from behind him reading his thoughts.

Joshua straightened up, turned around and said, "of course not." "I need you to cut his head off with the saw now." "Is he dead." "Are you retarded, look at him," man replied. Josh looked down at Masterson. The flesh from his face was gone, the eyes were gone and there where the nose holes but no nose, and you could see his skull and some hair. The rest of the body looked like a giant raw steak.

As Josh was looking down in horror, Masterson's body jumped up at him all of the sudden so Masterson's body and Josh were face to face. Josh started running the other way yelling. "Josh hold on," Man said laughing. "I made the body jump at you," he said in hysterics, "I was just fuckin with you." "Yeah, eat shit Caspiel," Josh shouted back thinking this was his best comeback.

"Now come over here and cut the fucking head off," Man said. Josh walked over still looking sternly. "Why are we cutting his head off again?" "Because I'm creating art, this is my creative time," Man said. Josh reluctantly picked up the saw and went over to Masterson and knelt down beside him.

He pushed down on his bloody forehead so the neck was more exposed. He picked a good spot on Masterson's neck, and started sawing. Now there was no way Masterson's heart was still pumping, so Josh was so surprised that while he was sawing he was getting spurted and covered in blood.

"No shit about getting bloody," Josh said. The head finally came off with another gush of blood through the neck hole. Josh looked over at man, panting. "Now stand up and pick up the fucking head", man commanded.

Josh stated to get up and grabbed the head with one of his hand and said, "what now." Man went over and picked up the crazy glue, then went over to Masterson and flipped his hand over palm up. He put some glue on the hand and said "now attached the head to the hand Josh." Josh did as he was told. As Josh was letting the glue set man got rid of all the rest of Masterson's clothes with a knife but left Masterson's priest's collar on, which was still on him under where Josh had cut. The glue had set.

"So what's with the head in the hand." "It's a Legion thing," man said.

Man motioned with his head and they went over and grabbed the rope. Each took an end, "You go left and I'll go right." Start tying the wrists with the rope the best you can." Josh got a rope and made a knot around the wrist as tight as he could. Man started wrapping the electrical tape around the wrist as well, about twenty times until he knew Masterson was secure.

He tossed the tape to Josh, and he did the same thing. Man put the middle of the rope over an air ventilation pipe that was closer to the edge of the building. Man walked back over to Masterson and said, "now, let's pick him up and throw him over the edge." Josh and man started picking up the body but it was a little lop sided because of man's height. They walked him over to the ledge that was over the church entrance.

Man motioned and they somehow twisted him around so Masterson was in a sitting position and his legs where dangling over the edge of the building. "Go get one of the wipes Josh," man said giggling." Josh went and got one of the wipes and went back over to them.

"Now Josh, I want you to stick it up his ass so he looks like he has a tail," man said laughing. Josh gave him an evil look and man gave him one back. Masterson was in a seated position and his ass was hanging over their side of the ledge. He reached over and stuck the handle of the wipe up Masterson's ass as quickly as he could. Man looked satisfied. There was metal sheets surrounding the edge of the roof and man took out a metal cutter sliced in to the hollow metal and made some jagged edges.

Man tucked in a length of rope into the cut in the metal and the rope caught on the edges. Man gave Josh the metal cutters "Josh just move down about three meters and do what I did." Joshua complied. "Now Josh, I want him lowered slowly," man said, "we don't want this falling apart." They lowered the body slowly so it was hanging over the entrance to the church. Man let go of the rope and he was gitty, clapping his little hands quickly in excitement.

"Come on Josh, let's go down and see it, let's go see my art." Man had Josh by the hand then let go because Josh wasn't moving fast enough, and started down the steps. "Come on Joshua," Man wined from the church floor.

Josh slowly made his way down the latter to piss man off. He got to the church floor. Man grabbed him by the hand again, "Come on," and he started to drag at him. Josh started into a light jog. They got outside. Josh was so afraid to look up. He was really getting noxious. "Oh you have to look, Josh you got to look," man said in amazement.

"Look at my art Josh, what we made Josh, it's wonderful," man said, still gitty. Josh covered his mouth and looked up at their macabre creation. It was horrific. Masterson was hanging in a crucifix position, head in hand with no face. The body looked like it had been whipped like Jesus had been, but much, much worse. But the freakiest thing wasn't that, or the wipe sticking out of his ass. It was the priest's collar. The white part in the collar was now blood red just as Crowley's had been. It looked very disturbing under the decapitated head cavity.

Man was starting to get angry. "Josh tell me you like it, tell me my art's good." Josh quickly turned his head to the side and puked all over the church steps. He stood up again and wiped the puke from his mouth and said sincerely "It's very nice man, is it your masterpiece?" "Almost," man said, "I can only think of a couple other of my pieces that transcend this one," he said with a smile still looking up. A huge wind came up out of nowhere and Masterson's body started eerily swaying.

Man took a deep breath and said "Well, let's get going then," and they both went down the step and started down the hill to the car.

"They should thoroughly enjoy that site in the morning," man said with his little childish giggle. "I'm proud of you Josh, man started, I think I'm going to start calling you killer." "No, Josh is fine, Josh is just fine," Joshua said sadly.

Man realized Josh was suffering some post traumatic stress and just trying to keep his mind together, so he left him alone. Josh was leaving a small trail of blood on the pavement behind him as they walked. "Where'd Azazel go," Josh asked. "Oh, you know Josh, he's always jumping from world to world, dimension to dimension."

They got to the car. Josh stripped down and grabbed the baby wipes and a towel and started wiping the blood and flesh off of him. He was mostly concerned with his face. He got most of it off and tossed the track suit in the dumpster they were parked beside. Josh got into his clothes and was shivering pretty bad from the shock. He did a couple of jumping Jacks to get the blood flowing again.

He got in the car and looked over at Man, "I don't think I'm going to be able to drive." Come on you pussy, man said annoyed, "I told you about our time restrictions, it's less than 2 hours to L.A." "I'll be feeding you the Strongbow for the ride to calm those nerves." Man passed over a Strongbow, Josh cracked it and took a swill and put it between his legs and lit a cigarette. Josh started the car and put her in reverse. "Man started putting the address of the hotel in the GPS and they were off again on their next little adventure.

Chapter 41

THEY WERE DRIVING and man gave Josh another Strongbow as Josh threw his last one out the T-bar roof. "So who's this next guy we're offing, I haven't gotten all the intel yet." "So how do you know a serial killer," Man asked. Immigrant song by Led Zeppelin was playing on the radio, (Ah, ah,

We come from the land of the ice and snow,

The hammer of the gods will drive our ships to new lands,

To fight the horde, singing and crying: Valhalla, I am coming!).

The wind was blowing through Josh's hair and he had a feeling of being normal for a few brief moments.

"His names Keith Atkins," Joshua started. "I didn't know he was a serial killer until Belial told me." "My Mom and I were living in Tacoma and my mother was into heroin real bad." "She was chasing the dragon, you know." "I still remember her dead eyes the whole time, there was absolutely no humanity in them, they were like a shark's eyes." "She was basically a vegetable most of the time but was still able to turned tricks to feed her habit and me." "I basically raised myself because my father sure didn't fucking want me."

"I still remember the day." "Mom was too sick to go out to meet her guy, so she had him come to our place." "She had only done that maybe two times before that, because she didn't want the guys around me at all." "There was a knock on the door and Mom told me I had to go read in my room for a bit." "You're not being punished Josh, mommy just is have a friend over for about a half an hour," she said as she stood up painfully from being dope sick.

"I went to my room, shut the door and grabbed my batman comics." "I heard a knock on the door, someone came in, and then the they turned the music up real loud." "Keith was shouting and slurring his words." "He was saying over and over, get naked and suck my cock bitch." "Then it was, now get up on the couch and bend over bitch." "Then there was hard slamming noises and I heard him slapping my mom." "Not to ruff Keith, I'm still sick, mom said." "Then the slamming and the slapping got harder." "TOO RUFF KEITH, my mom screamed."

"You think that's ruff bitch, try this out," he said "Mom started screaming again, then it stopped and I heard this load gurgling." "Choke on your own blood bitch," Keith said furiously. "I ran out to try and help her." "I saw Keith still fucking her from behind, he had a huge knife in his hand." "I saw my mother," bent over the top of the couch and blood was squirting from her neck and she was still gurgling." "He then noticed me, looking over with a look of pure hate at me." "He started to push himself off of mom to come at me." "I ran back in my room to the window." "I flung it open and dove out head first."

"I kinda landed on my head and was stunned, but I got up and ran as fast as I could without looking back." "Come back here you little shit, I heard from behind." "My mom had no friends in the neighborhood." "I knew my school wasn't open so I started running for the food bank, which was the only other place I knew to go." "I went through someone's yard and jumped the fence to get to the next street over and ran to the right and the food bank was just up a bit and left around the corner."

"I finally got enough courage to look back but there was no one there." "I didn't know what time it was so I didn't know if there would be anyone out." "I rounded the corner and saw three people out front of the food bank, smoking." "There was a woman and two men." "I ran up and clung on to the woman and put my head in her stomach panting, and then I puked." "She picked me up without saying a word and ran with me across the road." "She opened the door to her apartment building, and brought me upstairs to her room and dropped my on her bed."

"What happen little one," she said, "what happened to you," she said while rubbing my back and petting my head." "I tried to get the words out still panting, but I couldn't." "Then all the sudden, it came out."

"My mom, she's dead, there was a guy on top of her at my house and I just saw blood coming from her neck." "Then I started to wail and sob, because I hadn't been able to up until then." "She hugged me

ZACHARIAH LEHMANN

for a bit, while I cried, then asked my name." "I calmed down a bite, and then I looked up at her and said, my name is Joshua, and I live at 451 Richardson Street."

"She lied me back on the bed and said I'll be right back baby, I'll just be out in the hall on the phone for a minute". "She left the apartment and went to the payphone in the hallway." "I assume she called 911." "Then he heard, hi yes I got a 12 or 13 year old boy hear, he's all shook up." "He said he left his place and that his mother had just been murdered." "There was a long pause." "Then she said my name is Anne Marie Maduro and I live at 357 George street." "The boy is safe here but he told me his name is Joshua and he lives at 451 Richardson, maybe you should go there first and see what happened." "Yeah, my apartment number is 17." "Ok please hurry, she said concerned and hung up."

"I was in the hall by then listening, she rushed over and grabbed me by the hand again and took me back to the bed and we lied down and she was spooning me as I started to cry again." "It will be ok, baby, the police are going right over to check on your momma." "You can call me Annie she said, and your safe with me as she stroked my head and kissed me on the cheek." "Just calm down the best you can baby, everything is going to be alright."

"But I knew everything wasn't alright, and I started balling again." "A little bit later there was a knock on the door." "A man and a women walked in and introduced themselves and said they were from social services." "You're not going to take him home are you," Annie said, "he's real shook up." "No ma'am the woman said, we're not even going to take him to the police station, he'll just come back to our office and we'll talk to him and find out what he saw and then we'll get him in a place where he's safe and where he can stay for awhile." "He can stay with me, Annie spoke up."

"Well we thank you for your concern ma'am, and I mean no offence but we just can't bring him back here." "You're not in a position to help anyone else now, you just have to take care of yourself." "Will you tell me where you put him so I can go talk to him and make sure he's ok, Annie said." "We'll try to get that information to you." "Thank you so much for taking him in, the man said as he lifted me out of the bed."

"They both left with me and I heard Annie saying, be safe baby Joshua, I hope for the best for you." "She knew social services wouldn't tell her where they were going to put me." "They got me back to the office, and I told them everything I saw." "I couldn't remember what the guy looked like, I guess my mind was blocking the image of his face."

"All I knew was that his name was Keith." "I ended up in a foster home after that." "They didn't even have a funeral for her because I heard while the adults were talking, that my father wouldn't pay for it." "I heard them saying that my father said, the filthy cunt doesn't deserve one." "My foster parents took me over to the Catholic Church." "The priest there asked my foster parents if they were ok to take care of me because the church had a school for boys in Seattle." "They said they were ok for the time being but they took the church's number just in case."

"The priest then asked them to leave us for about an hour." "We went and sat down in the front pew." "The priest was very nice." "We talked about my mom for a while, and I told him all my best memories of her and he didn't even ask me about the drugs she was doing." "We were sitting there and he told me to look up at Jesus."

"He started praying for my mom calling her a child of God and saying that she is in a wonderful place now." "I know you miss her Josh, he said, she misses you so much too, but you will see her again in heaven when it's your time." "I didn't really understand what he was saying, all I could figure out was that I probably wasn't going to see my mom again for a very long time."

"The most important thing for you to do now is to be strong and behave for my foster parents because they were nice enough to take me in and take care of me." "The priest said he would come in and check on me from time to time." "He was good on his word, he came to see me about six times a year and we would always have good long talks and he made me feel like I was a special person." "I loved him, his name was Father Dyer."

"I moved foster homes a few times and he was transferred to another diocese and we lost touch, Josh told man." "So I guess he had been offing prostitutes before that and for a couple years after." "Then he decided to find God again and started working at a shelter helping street people in L.A." "I still can't remember his face, and I know there's going to be some bad flashbacks when I see it." "Man passed Josh another can, as he threw his last one out the roof." "I think that one hit the car behind us," man said laughing, as the car behind them started honking." "Yeah I'm sure it will be pretty fucked up to see him again," man said, "but there will be no salvation from the Nazarene for this man." "He will burn and suffer in the in the lowest circle of hell." "He's ours now," man said with a big grin.

ZACHARIAH LEHMANN

Chapter 42

"SO WHAT'S THE plan." "We'll I got the info now," man said. "So Keith works at St. Matthew's." "It's like a half shelter and half church in a bad part of downtown." "He works the three to eleven shift so we'll get him right after work." "We'll go down to the strip around 10 and pick up a working girl to pick him up." "I rented a room down there, it's real seedy." "When she brings him up we'll do our thing."

"And what's our thing this time," Josh asked." "Josh, you know I don't like ruining the surprise," man said sternly in his little voice. "I thought he was born again," Josh asked. "Yeah, we'll make sure he won't be able to resist her, man said." "I said he quit killing, not having sex." "You just assume sex and violence go together," man told Josh. "I don't want to get into semantics," Josh said, "can you pass me another can."

They got to L.A. just after 1 am. They got into the hotel and got settled. Josh continued drinking and smoking weed. No more PCP, he gave it up for man. He was man's little bitch and had to do whatever he said. But he knew it would all be over in a couple of days. "Josh will go back to his great life created by Lucifer, and more importantly they guaranteed he would be with his sweet Jade again," he thought with a smile. He was thinking of Jade.

That's what Josh did with his downtime, and get trashed. Man just sat in the big chair and stared out the window at the dark sky. Josh couldn't understand it, there was nothing to look at. It's not as if you can see stars anymore in L.A. He sat there just staring and kind of bobbing back and forth to the classical music on his I pod. Josh crashed on his bed and was almost instantly asleep.

He woke up at five pm the next day. Man was gone. Josh didn't care. He turned on the T.V and lied in bed for about another hour and a half, watching reruns of six feet under on cable. He then turned it to KTLA news and they were talking about the murder in San Diego."

"In all my years as a reporter, I have never seen a murder such as this, It's absolutely horific." The reporter started, "such desecration of the church, and of a human body, is very unsettling." "We cannot show you the murder scene, but I understand pictures were on the internet for about forty five minutes before they were pulled." "From what we've heard, the victim, Father Masterson was basically in retirement but still had some small duties during the masses, and was also volunteering in the community."

"You would think something like this was done by pure evil, by Lucifer himself." "But this act was perpetrated by his fellow priest," the reporter continued. "After discovering the body, the police went into the Church rectory to check on the rest of the clergy." "Inside they found the bodies of four Filipino nuns."

"From there they went to Father Simon's room." "Father Simon is the head priest for St. John's Catholic Church." "In his room they found the priest passed out, intoxicated on his bed." "Police said that some of the material used to display Father Masterson's body were found in the priest's room, along with the knife that was used to slit the nun's throats." "We have footage of police leading father Simon down the steps of the rectory."

"There was a boy," Simon screamed. "A boy of pure evil that was in my church yesterday." "He did this," Simon screamed seeming like he was out of his mind." "He was not a boy at all," he continued as the officers threw him in the back of the cruiser. "But it wasn't a boy at all," "It was legion," Simon said as they slammed the back door shut.

"Right now we have Doctor Samual Smith from the university of California, Berkley with us." "Doctor Smith, what would make a man of the cloth do what he did, to his fellow children of God." "What kind sickness are we dealing with here?" The reported asked.

"Well, Smith said with a sad sigh, we're dealing with someone in the advance stages of severe mental Illness, more than likely a case of schizophrenia." "I can't speculate on what was going through his mind except for that this Priest harbored an incredible hatred for the Catholic Church, and God himself."

ZACHARIAH LEHMANN

Josh turned the T.V. off and sat up in bed. His stomach was killing him and he was holding himself, rocking back and forth. He finally got up and shock himself off, and went to the bathroom to get ready. When he came out man was there. "So you really weren't too happy with that priest eh," Josh said. "What, were you watching the news," man asked and Josh nodded. "I got that cocksucker good didn't I," man said laughing. "You sure did," Josh said a little frightened.

"I got what we needed," man changed the subject, "it wasn't much," and he pointed over at the table. On the table was the electrical tape from San Diego, two pairs of steel handcuffs, a wooden Spalding baseball bat, and a very, very large scalpel." "We'll ok then," Josh didn't bother asking what they were going to do with the things, but he figured it was going to get real bloody again.

Chapter 43

THEY HEADED DOWN at the strip and got there about quarter to ten. "Now Josh here's the story when we talk to the whore, Man started." "It's basically the truth of what happen to your mom, but I'm you son who you let tag along to avenge his grandmother's death. "We'll tell her Keith got off on a technicality because the police fucked up and lost the DNA evidence, so we have to avenge your mother ourselves." "We just need her to pick him up, take him to us at the hotel, get the cuffs on and secure him to the bed." "That's it."

"If she wants to stay for the festivities or walk, either way is good." "Did you understand Josh or do you want me to repeat myself," man said sarcastically. "I understand," Josh said back sternly. "Good, man said with a smile, use that rage on Keith." Josh slowed down a bit and they were both surveying the ladies. One shouted "nice car." Another hooker said, "Fuck dude, you shouldn't have that kid down here," and was coming towards the car so Josh speed up a little.

They went for about another 20 seconds and man said "start stopping, I found the her." Josh stopped the car, put it in first and turned it off. "You see the redhead up ahead," and pointed up the street a bit. "Yeah," Josh said. "That's her." Man said. Josh did a double take. She was tall, about 5 10". She looked like an eighteen year old Julian Moore, just stunning. She was wearing a nice white tank top and a pair of daisy dukes that showed half her ass, and stiletto heels.

Josh started the car up and they moved up beside the girl. She was listening to her I pod, "I wonder if she was listening to classical," Josh though stupidly. She looked over, and Josh gave her a quick nod and she made her way over to the firebird. "Oh what a cute little boy, I love his outfit," she started. Man was just there looking up at her with a stupid grin on his face. "Hey what's your name," Josh said in a friendly voice. "Vicki," she replied. "Hey Vikki, I'm Josh, I just need to talk to you for a minute." "Yeah sure thing," she said sweetly. "I'm not a psycho who wants to have sex with you while my kid whatch's or something."

"We do think you could help us out though." "Sure what's up," she said. "We need for you to do something for us that doesn't involve sex, and you will be well compensated." "Josh pulled out 10 hundred dollar bills and fanned them at her. "Well," I'm going to have to know what that something is."

Josh looked up the street and saw a seedy strip club. "Well can I take you for a drink up there and we can talk about it." "Sure," she said. "Hop in the back bud," Josh said to man. Man jumped into the tiny backseat. Vikki got in and they were off to the bar. They walked in and made their way over to a booth. "So what's up," Vikki asked.

The waitress walked over. "You can't have that boy in the bar." "Ma'am, we're just here for a quick drink and then I'm taking him right to bed." "We'll be here less than 10 minutes and we'll tip very well." "Ok, what ONE drink each can I get you." Vikki spoke up, "G&T." Josh knew they wouldn't have Strongbow so he ordered a Bud. "So what's up," Vikki repeated. Josh proceeded to tell her the story and the details diabolical plan.

"What a fucker," Vikki said with hate in her eyes. "Yeah I'll do it," "and I'll stick around to fuck that cunt up too." "Excellent, Josh said and passed her the wad of hundreds." "It was about ten forty and it would take about 10 minutes to get to the shelter. They got in the firebird and were on their way. They got to there and parked across the street. "Ok Vikki, you might have to try hard because he might not be too interested at first." "Well I'm an actress during the day you know, I've been on Young and the Restless like three times," she said gloating. "Wow, three times Vikki, that's awesome, so you shouldn't have a problem with this then." "His name is Keith but pretend that you don't know him of course," man said.

"When he gets outta work he always walks down the road that way," and man pointed. "So you should stand over thereby that side of the building to catch him." "Then just take him to that hotel," man said pointing. "Tell the front desk guy you're going to room two forty nine, that's all you have to say."

Vikki looked down at Man with a stunned look on her face. "Why was this child talking like an adult, and why was she taking orders from him," she thought. "OK", she finally said, popped out of the car and headed across the street." "I have faith in you, we'll see you back at the hotel," Josh said. "K," Vikki yelled while crossing the street. Joshed turned the car around and headed for the hotel.

Chapter 44

THEY WALKED IN the front door and nodded to the Desk clerk as they walked by. The clerk didn't flinch, no reaction. He looked like he was having a bad herpies outbreak on his lips and that it would hurt to talk.

They went up the stairwell to the second floor and went all the way to the end of the hall to the last room on the right. The hotel was disgusting, there were actually blood stains on the walls. The carpets looked like they hadn't been cleaned since the eighties. There was no one in the halls but there were some very strange noises from some of the rooms as they passed by them.

They got to the room and it was equally disgusting. The bed was barely made and you could tell that sheets hadn't been cleaned. There was a large cum stain on the comforter and a horrible picture of what looked to be a Mexican princess on the wall. Josh and the princess's eyes met and it looked like her eyes were following him as he walked around.

"So what now," Josh said, he had brought a couple of cans in with him. "We gotta wait in the washroom," man said, "we don't want him to see us when he first comes in." Josh cracked one of his Strongbow and said "I like Vikki, she's got spunk." "Do you want to fuck her when we're done Josh, because I can arrange that," Man said. "No, I don't think I'll be in the mood," Josh said sadly.

"Try to stop thinking about Jade," Man said, "it's just fucking you up in the head." About ten minutes later, they heard the door to the room open. "Come on baby," Vikki was saying, "I want to ride you like the stallion you are." Keith was laughing.

"We'll this sounds like it's going to be fun," Keith replied. "Just you wait," Vikki said. "I'm going to suck your cock for a while and ride you to town," Vikki said with a playful laugh. "Alright then, I'm in," Keith replied. "Ok strip down and lie on your back," Keith complied and laid down on the bed. "Well, it's Keith right," Vikki said. "Right." "Well Keith, I got this bondage fetish from my daddy." "He used to tie me up and rape me when I was seven." "But now I like to tie other people up." Don't worry, just your hands, not your feet." "It will make me way more horny, which will make you experience so much better," Vikki said with a wink. "No worries," Keith said and put his arms out, towards the bed corners.

She grabbed two sets of hand cuffs and attached them to Keith's wrists, and each one of the bedposts. "Not so tight," he said, and Vikki loosened them a bit. "Are you ready," Vikki said. "Ready as I'll ever be," Keith responded in anticipation.

All of the sudden Josh and man came out of the bathroom. Josh had the electrical tape, jumped on the bed, grabbed Keith's legs started taping them up. "What the fuck is this, Keith said, are you the fucking police." Then man jumped up on the bed and stood on Keith's chest. He looked down on him. "No we're not the cops, if we were the cops, you'd be safe right now," man said with a smile.

"Get off of me," Keith said with hardly any breath in him. Man jumped up and down on Keith's chest and he started heaving. Man looked down at him again. "We're here to destroy everything and ruin your life," "God sent us," man said in a monotone voice.

Josh turned the radio up to drown out the noise. Ace of spades by motor head was playing (if you like to gamble ill tell you I'm your man, you win some loose some, it's all the same to me). Josh looked over and said I know you, do you remember me. "No I don't know who the fuck you are," Keith said. "Listen dude, I haven't done anything, I work at a homeless shelter for Christ sake." "This is the first time I tried to pick a hooker in six years, what is she your sister or something?" "And who's the psycho little kid," Keith asked. "Yeah you wouldn't remember me Keith, we just meet briefly in Tacoma in 2001."

"You were over at my house VISITING my mother." "I heard her screaming from my room." "I came out to try and save her, but you had already slit her throat and I came out to you on top of her, still fucking her while she bled out."

"You saw me and tried to come after me, you were going to kill me too." "I jumped out my bedroom window and ran, I guess you couldn't get your fucking fat ass out the window to chase me." Keith just laid there with a blank expression on his face. "Now look at me Keith, I'm a psychopathic killer because of all the childhood trauma you caused me." "My friends and I are your executioners."

"Vikki walked over to the corner of the room and grabbed the bat." "We'll Keith, aren't you going to insist it wasn't you, tell me that it was a bad time in your life but that you have found Jesus," Josh shouted loudly. "No," Keith said in a monotone voice, I know you are going to kill me, i'm not going to give you the satisfaction." "Yeah, fucking right we're going to kill you motherfucker," Vikki said from behind Josh, then lifted the bat above her head and walked over to the bed. She screamed and gave Keith three vicious shots to the head. Keith yelled out, "oh fuck." Vikki turned looked over at the other side of the bed at man, she was panting and giving man very crazy stare.

Man nodded at her, and then she just unleashed all her inner hatred on Keith. She started screaming in rage and was bludgeoning Keith all over his body. After about three minutes Man shouted "Stop," and Vikki dropped the bat and went over to the couch and fell on it face down panting. Then gave out an ear piercing scream into the cushion. Josh looked down at him, the blood was covering his face from cuts from the blows. His eyes were blinking rapidly and he was convulsing. He started choking and then he spit up his own teeth and was silent and still for a moment.

Vikki got up and walked back over to the bed with the same psychotic look in her eyes, and then spit in Keith's bloody face. "Did you like that you fucking cock sucker," Vikki yelled as she got in Keith's lifeless face. It was becoming clear that Vikki had grown up with a horrible home life and had a serious issues with men.

Man walked over and handed Josh the scalpel. "Now cut is dick off and end this Josh," he said sternly. Josh turn away and then turned back to Keith. He paused for a minute then said without any feeling, "This is what you get for killing my Mom and fucking me up."

"Come on Josh, pull it together, finish it," man said. "Yeah get that fucking cunt Josh," Vikki screamed. Keith had a hard on, I guess because the blood from his heart was pumping so fast. Josh got himself together and pulled up Keith's scrotum. He made the incision under

Keith's testicles so they would be attached when it was severed. Josh then started cutting and trying to saw it off with the scalpel.

He looked over at Keith's face. It was just frozen in a look of absolute horror and pain that Josh would never forget. There was a little wimping from Keith, but he just didn't have the life in him to shout out. On the sheets the puddle of blood had started accumulating around his groin. "Finish it," man shouted.

Josh continued to saw and in about ten seconds Keith's penis was severed, his body still convulsing, Josh guessed from the severe pain and shock. The groin cavity was now gushing blood and Keith then just stopped moving. Josh looked down at Keith's penis and said shaking "what the fuck do I do with this."

"Vikki open his mouth," man instructed. She bent over Keith and complied. "Now Josh, stick his fucking cock in his own mouth." "Josh pushed the penis and testicles into Keith's mouth. Keith's testicles fell out of his scrotum when Josh stopped pushing and a clear liquid was running down Keith's chin over the blood.

"See Josh, another piece of my art," man said happily. "Do you like my masterpiece Vikki," man asked. "I love it man," Vikki said fully satisfied just like she ate a huge meal, and sat down on the couch and lit a cigarette. Josh wasn't as calm, still vibrating from the whole ordeal. "Vikki, we bid you adieu, please leave now," man said calmly. "Well, thanks for the money guys, and thanks for letting me join in, that was fucking fun." "Here," Vikki said giving Josh her card, "If you boys ever need to get some frustration on someone again, or if you need to get fucked Josh, shoot me a text."

She stopped as she was walking out. "What about DNA," she asked. "Don't worry about it," man said, "I got it covered." Vikki knew this boy wasn't human and she believed him. "Well, so long," she said, and rushed out the door and down the hall.

Josh walked over to Keith again, and looked down at him with his own penis hanging out of his mouth. "Why did you have to kill my mom," Josh said still whimpering. "I needed her."

"Get yourself together you fucking little girl," man shouted at Josh. He then grabbed Josh by the hand and led him out of the room and down the hall. About half way down the hall he broke from man's grasp and started walking ahead of him in silence. They walked down the stairs and were passing by the front desk. Josh, and Vikki for that matter, had blood covering them, but the desk clerk barely gave them a glance. Josh though "I guess this was a normal occurrence for him to see."

Man was behind Josh and stopped at the desk, pulled a hundred dollar bill out of his pocket and handed it to the clerk. "This is for the inconvenience of the cleaning." The clerk just put it in his pocket went in the back room to grab some new sheets, the carpet cleaner, bleach and a brush. He put up a back in five minutes sign on the desk, and started up the stairs to two forty nine.

They started towards the car. "Now Josh," man started, "think of what I'm about to say as like marriage councelling for us," man said with a chuckled. "So Josh, when you show weakness and break down emotionally when we are killing someone," "I try very hard to be supportive of you, and try to help you out of your shell." "But Josh," man said very kindly, "when you act like that, it makes me feel like I want to kill you slowly, then dismember you, and then rent a boat and take you out to feed you to the sharks." "Now Josh, how does what I said make you feel," man said concerned.

"Fuck you," Josh replied, "I'm getting better." "See that's why I think our relationship is in trouble Josh, because of the anger manner in which you respond to me." "Go fuck yourself, I didn't puke this time, did I." "No Josh, you didn't," man shouted. "But showing weakness like that, especially in front of a women who is much weaker than you, is troubling." "I should have had her cut his fucking dick off, it would have been less dramatic," man shouted at him. "I know," Josh said frustrated.

"Did you see the look in her eyes," Josh continued, "that chick has some major issues." "I wonder if that story was true about her dad tying her up and raping her." "It was," man said, "that's why I picked her." "She was the most attractive and the most fucked up one down on the strip." "What about the DNA, you're you going to blame her for it?" "No," man said, "I said I wouldn't and I'm a man of my word," man started. "Schwarzenegger has been a real pain in the ass for us lately." man said. "He's just not adapting to our plan." "He was at a function at the Governor's mansion tonight and they'll be a one hundred fifty people swearing he was there, but DNA doesn't lie now does it Josh," man said smiling.

"I'm going to make it into a fag suicide pact that went wrong," man said giggling. Josh started laughing, "that's fucking classic." "It's already done," man responded. "The Governors going to jail and then down with us, that's if he doesn't kill himself first, which is a definite possibility with that faggot." "Either way," man said.

ZACHARIAH LEHMANN

Chapter 45

THEY GOT TO the car and Josh pulled out of the shitty parkade. "We're going back to San Francisco now right," Josh asked. "Yeah, just head for your place," man said cracking a can and lighting a joint for him. "Where just going to hang out there and I'll let you get some rest some rest, because, well, man continued, our final adventure is going to blow your fucking mind." Josh just shook his head. He was never a patient person, and waiting to find out what was going to happen instead of controlling his own destiny drove him fucking batty. But he bit his tongue and didn't say anything.

They pulled into the driveway about six am. Josh turned the car off, got out and walked quickly into the house not even looking at man. He ran upstairs and collapsed on his bed, and with some deep breaths was unconscious in about thirty seconds.

Chapter 46

OSH WOKE UP at three the next day. He thought back on the last couple days and the sickness feeling inside of him had lessened. He was becoming desensitized to his new life. He jumped up and got in the shower and got ready. The sun shone on him threw his window. It was like he hadn't seen it in years. He went downstairs to start his day with a can and joint. He looked over into his living room and all the boys were there. Belial, man, Azazel, and Astaroth, had all made them comfortable on his furniture and were just staring at him in silence.

"Come sit down Josh," Belial said. "Can I just grab a can, this looks like it might get intense." "Go ahead," man said in his little voice. Josh went into the kitchen and grabbed the can, "why were they all here, this can't be a good thing," he thought with his heart starting to beat out of his chest.

Josh returned and there was his chair in the middle of the floor positioned facing them, like he was going for a job interview. Josh sat and looked them all in the eye. "You've done a wonderful job those past two kills, their souls are both with us now," Belial started. "But this is where things get a little more interesting." "Jades in town Josh." "Really," Josh said with excitement, when can I see her." "Very soon," Astaroth said.

"Do you know the intense feeling you've been feeling about her since you met," Belial started. "Yeah," Josh said in agreement." "We'll that's because when she met you, she put a love spell on you." "Those feelings you have for her aren't real."

"No, no, no, that's bullshit, it's very real," Josh said defending himself. "It's the spell Josh, your feelings for her are artificial." Josh wouldn't believe it, couldn't believe it. "And Josh she's sick, she got into the heroin real bad when she got back into town."

"She's just not there mentally or physically anymore." "She has about twelve hours before the drugs take her."

Josh went over to the window, started crying and rubbing his face. "How do I know this is the truth," Josh shouted, "you guys always fucking lie." "Well you're going to see her very soon, so you'll see for yourself." "And the story gets better Josh," man said with a chuckle. "You're going to have to kill her, and eat her heart to get rid of the love spell before she dies, or for the rest of your life you'll have those feelings for her which will consume you and eventually destroy you." Josh was now laughing, he was losing his mind quickly.

"YOU WANT ME TO EAT MY FUCKING GIRLFRIEND'S HEART," Josh shouted. "Oh the drama Josh, and you thought of Belial as such a queen, look at you now you fucking pussy," man said. "You have no choice, now, go fucking do it," man shouted at him. Josh walked out of the room and into the kitchen to grab another can, and he was trembling pretty bad.

He tried to say something to them, but his voice was too shaky and he stopped. "She's pregnant too, Josh." "What," Josh shouted back. "Yeah, what can I tell you Josh, she's a whore," Belial said. "Don't fucking say that," he replied. "So she put a love spell on you and then fucked another guy and now is having his baby." "Nice eh," Belial said. "I can't fucking believe this," Josh said panting.

"Yeah, go eat her heart Josh," Azazel said, "it will make you feel better," and they all started laughing, Azazel squealing. He walked back in the room and shouted, "and you really think I am physically capable of eating Jade's heart." "We realize you'll still be under the spell until you actually eat it, so when it's time to do the deed, we will take over." "Take over, what does that mean," Josh asked. "We will possess you Josh, you won't even remember it."

"And Josh we want the fetus, you'll have to cut it out and bring it to us." Josh had tears running down his face. "Motherfucking Pussy," Man shouted at him. "Josh she's going to die anyways, this is a mercy killing," Belial reassured him. "Don't you want her to feel no more pain." Josh was looking out the window again and blankly said, "Yes." "Try to take comfort in the fact that you have no choice in the matter."

He knew killing Jade was inevitable, and he also knew that his deeds for these fucks wouldn't end after Jade as they had promised. "Oh, this will be the last one," Astaroth said reading Josh's thoughts, his viper shot at Josh trying to bite at him. "Where is she," Josh said. "Oh, she's at the heroin hotel downtown," Belial said handing him a card with the address on it.

The place was called The Twilight, the card said Great hourly rates, and had the address. "So we'll be in touch after it's done to discuss the end of the pact and the life you've always dreamed of Josh," Belial said with a smile. Belial, Azazel, and Astaroth just kind of dissipated. Man walked by Josh and said, "do it pussy," as he walked out the patio door, Josh started following him and shouted, "you're not going to fucking help me." "Nope," man said and jumped over the patio railing and down into the revene.

Chapter 47

JOSH JUST STOOD there for about ten minutes, lit a cigarette and tried his best to control his thoughts and emotions. He was pacing again. It was about five forty five pm, so he had till about five am the next day, but he wanted to see Jade so bad, to see if what they said was true. He was already dressed and ready.

But he couldn't go before he was fucked up, that was just a given. He just wasn't strong enough to see her like that if he was sober. Josh shot back three triples of Balvenie, and was reeling from the burning in his mouth. It was now about six fifteen. Josh put on his Giants cap and his sunglasses, grabbed three cans from the fridge and four joints and headed off downtown.

Chapter 48

JOSH PULLED INTO a parking garage, about a ten minute walk to the motel. He couldn't park the firebird down there, it would be gone a minute after he walked in the door. He started walking and cracked a can. "The Water's edge," by Seven Mary Three started playing in his head, (don't go there I heard her say, you can't stomach what your gonna see). He hadn't stopped thinking about Jade, he started to light jog because he wanted to get there faster. He jogged for about two minutes and then a big vagrant came out of the alley while he was running by. Josh was dressed pretty well so he stuck out like a sore thumb.

"Hey, mister, what you running from, what you got to hide from." He heard him starting to run behind him. "Hey mister, come back here and give me your fucking money." "Josh remembered the scalpel he had in his pocket for Jade." He pulled the big blade out and turned to him, "come on motherfucker, you want some of this," Josh said while lunging at him.

The vagrant saw the blade and quickly turned the other way running. Josh turned back towards the motel and started running. He got there and ran in the door and quickly slowed. As he was puffing from running he was looking around.

It was really bad. The fat female clerk was looking at him like, who the fuck is this guy. He looked into what Josh guessed was the lounge. There we're two guys in there sixties, and this tiny little eighteen year old girl who looked like she weighed about seventy five pounds. They were all passed out. The girl still had the needle in her arm and puke all over her chest. "Not a good sign," Josh thought. He reached in his pocket and got out the card Belial gave him with the address and room number.

He looked on the back of the card, room seventeen was written. "You look like a fucking cop," the clerk said. "We'll I'm not a cop, you'll just have to trust me on that one," Josh said. "Where's room seventeen," he asked. She didn't answer him, just stared as he walked by. He walked down the dark hallway to the left of her. There was only one small light on in the huge hallway. He looked ahead and there we're a few people passed out face down in front of their doors. They were too high to make it inside.

Chapter 49

HE LOOKED AT the door beside him and it was thirteen. Then he heard something start to come up from behind him. Josh didn't look back, speed up, went down two more doors and ran in the room, turned around, and locked the deadbolt. He stood there for a second with his head against the door, afraid to turn around. He heard three distinct bangs on the door behind him.

He turned around and jade jumped in his arms crying and laughing, "Oh Joshua," she cried more, "I was just going to die if I didn't see you again," she said in his ear as he held her up. Josh stroked her hair, "It's ok baby, it's ok," he said and starting to cry a bit himself. "How did you get here, how did you know where I was." "They told me," Josh said.

"Come and sit on the bed with me," she said dragging him by the hand forward. He went with her and they sat down. She looked over at him, grabbed him and pulled him in and gave him such an innocent kiss. "I missed you so much." "I love you so much Jade," he said laughing and crying at the same time. He looked over at her and she definitely not look well.

She was wearing a dirty tee shirt with blood on it, and she had track marks up and down the veins in her arms and between her fingers. Her face was really thin and she had two black circles under her eyes. She also had a small baby bump under her shirt. Josh stood up and looked down at her in shock. She looked up, and said, "Yeah baby, we got to talk." Josh sat down beside her again and just held her for a bit. "You know hunny, you can tell me anything," he said sincerely and expecting something very, very bad.

She broke his embrace, stood up and started pacing with a stunned look on her face. "Yeah something bad happened," she said not looking at him. She keep on pacing. "While you were away, while you we're away from me Josh, they took me away," Jade started.

"I wasn't on earth, but it looked like earth at the same time." "I know, I've been there too," Josh said remembering when he was on the church roof with Masterson. "Yeah it's a different Astro plane, they can take us there through their portals," she said. "I was there and I was alone." "I was in a city I've never been before and there was a blood red sky." "There was no time, at least I couldn't feel any concept of time." "I was wondering around the city for what felt like for days or months, or I don't know."

"I went to the museum and the city art gallery, but the painting all seemed to be distorted and the figures in the painting's started jumping out at me, so I ran out of there screaming." "I just keep on wandering, you know, looking for people." "I was just walking aimlessly, and I ended up in what seemed to be a bad part of town." "I just kept walking, there was no one around and I didn't know what else to do."

"I passed this alley, and I saw three black figures standing in front of a drum that was on fire." "I couldn't make out the faces through the vapor above the fire." "I started to walk towards them because they were the only people I had seen up too that point," she said starting to cry again. "As I got closer, I started to make out the figures." "It was Belial, Azazel, and Astaroth." "I turned to run back out to the street but now they were behind me blocking the entrance to the Alley." "I asked them what they wanted with me and if they were taking me back to the real world." "Eventually," Astaroth said, "but we're going to have some fun with you first."

"I started to back up." "Where are you going, there's no place to go unless you're going to climb that wall," Astaroth said laughing." "Your life's worth shit now, you have no hope," Belial said. "I asked if they were going to kill me." "No Jade, that would be too easy, plus we still need you, Belial said," "But after we're finished with you, you'll wish you were dead, Azazel told me with a squeal."

"They started to approach me." "I turned and tried to run even though there was nowhere to go." "One of them grabbed me from behind and threw me forwards to the ground." "I looked up and the three of them were standing above me." "Have you ever had three cocks at once Jade, we're going to fill all your holes, Belial said laughing." "I jumped up and tried to run between them." "Belial grabbed me by the throat and threw me back down to the ground." "Azazel was behind me and started to rip my clothes off."

"They continued to gang rape me for what seemed like an hour, first one by one, then all together." "I don't remember much, just the pain, the intense pain and their comments as they assaulted me."

"When I finally came to afterwards, Belial was carrying me like a baby towards a portal that had appeared down the street." "I couldn't move from the pain I was in." "I felt something in my stomach, a horrible lump." "We passed through the portal and I ended up here."

"Belial threw me on the bed." "You're going to see Joshua very soon Jade." "I'm going to send someone in to help you with the pain, but you will not be able to leave until Joshua comes for you." "Belial exited through the door." "I couldn't move or get up to try and get away," she said with tears coming down her face. "About five minutes later, that fat fucking bitch of a desk clerk came in." "We're cooking up Jade, I wouldn't want you to miss out." "She had a needle in her hand, the end was dripping, and heroin was coming out."

"She walked over, I tried to get up again but I was totally immobile." "The bitch was smiling and bent down and stuck the needle in my arm, slowly pushing the heroin in." "I just remember letting out a hug breath and slowly went into a higher state." "The pain was fading quickly." "I was just lying there trying to take it all in." "I finally fell unconscious again." "When I woke up, I was still in this bed." "I turned over and puked on the floor." "My vision was blurry, but I could move now."

"I got up and stumbled to the door and started down the hall towards the front door." "As I passed the office, that bitch clerk came out from the side door and clocked me with a vicious punch to the temple." "I was down again but still conscious." "She grabbed me by the hair and started dragging me back towards the room." "She lifted me up with such strength it wasn't human, and threw me back on the bed and shot me up again with another syringe."

"Again that feeling of happiness, I felt all warm and fuzzy again, and I forgot of all the bad things, I was having an out of body experience." "I was flying above the city and then I remember nothing."

"I woke up again so dope sick." "It was night now, and the building was silent." "I went to the door and slowly looked out down the hall."

ZACHARIAH LEHMANN

"The fat bitch was standing in the hallway." "I ran back into the room and went over to try to open the window, but it was nailed shut."

"She came up behind me and stuck me again, and I fell back into the bed." "When I came to the next time, there was a syringe waiting for me on the bedside table." "I didn't even try to escape then, I knew it wasn't going to happen." "I gave up Josh, and I shot myself up because I was craving it so bad now, that feeling of happiness and void of not being in the real world."

"A couple of days in I noticed my stomach was in a lot of pain." "I looked down and the baby bump was there Josh, and my stomach muscles were rippling." "That continued until today." "That's who I thought you were, that fat bitch coming to shoot me up." "Oh my God Josh, I was so happy and jumped at you." "You've come to save me haven't you, and now we're going to be together forever, right Josh," she said giving him a big hug.

"Let's just get out of this shitty town Josh, go as far away as we can, and never look back." "I wish we could," Josh said, but I don't think they're going to let us go that easily."

"So what the fuck are we going to do Josh," she said angrily, "we've got to get the fuck out of here, I'm not staying here," she screamed, and lied back down in bed. Josh bent over and kissed her on the forehead. "I just want this fucking thing out of me, I want this thing out of me and you inside of me Josh."

"I'm getting really sick from the drugs again, Josh." "I'm so afraid of what it is inside of me, I'm so scared, "she said as she buried her head into his stomach. "Make love to me Josh, I know you'll feel so much better than the heroin," she said pleading. "And then help get this fucking thing out of me." Josh just looked at her with a weak smile, his mind was completely blank.

He knew there was no way out of this. He started crying again, "while you were gone a lot of bad things happened," "I killed those people from my past that Belial talked about when I sold my soul." "The whole time I was thinking of you, the image of you in my mind was the only thing that keep me going, that and they guaranteed that I would see you again." Josh didn't mention that he knew about the love spell, he didn't want to upset her and put her on the defensive.

"So is it over now, you've done everything they've asked of you, haven't you," Jade questioned. "I still have one more kill Jade, I just had to see you before I did it, then I'll come back for you and we will be free," Josh said lying. "Well then go finish it Josh, finish it so we can leave all of this shit behind us."

"But be with me before you go Josh, I need to feel you inside of me and I know the pain will go away." She looked over and gave him a smile and started to undo his pants. She started to go down on him. Josh tried to concentrate on getting hard, it was the last thing on his mind but he had to do it, so he blocked out his sadness.

When he was hard she got up an undressed. She jumped on the bed on all fours because she knew that was the way he liked it. "No hunny, just lie on you back," he said, I want to be gentle with you tonight." "You've been through too much." She smiled at him and lied on her back with her legs bent and up in the air.

"Take me Joshua, I know as soon as your inside of me, I'll feel extacy," Jade said with her face brightening up. Joshua got up and undressed. He got on top of her with is elbows on each side of her head. "Do you want me to go down on you, are you wet," he said trying to fight back the tears. "No I'm so wet baby, just get in there," she said.

Josh entered her and she let out a long moan. She didn't say anything, there was just a huge smile on her face and her eyes were closed like she was enjoying every second. Josh got in and suffered though the first dryness and after three stokes, she was so wet she was flowing. Josh started pumping and there was no friction. She was sloppy wet and he could hear her wetness with each stroke.

He grabbed with his arms under her knees and with her legs above her head and started pumping hard. Jade was screaming, "Oh yeah baby, all the pains gone now, harder, HARDER," she wailed. Josh complied and she was just in a trance from him fucking her, just closed eyes and a smile as she jumped every time he entered her.

The light above Jade's bed started flickering like a strobe light, making everything look like it was in slow motion. Josh started to hear the buzzing in his ears and he pulled out and covered his ears to try and muffle the sound, but it was in his head. He fell onto the floor, still holding his ears from the screeching audio pain.

"What's wrong, get back inside of me," Jade demanded. He slowly got up and went over to his pants to grab the scalpel. He held it behind his back, and started walking back towards the bed.

"Yeah hunny," Jade said, "come here." He went back and got on top of her and hid the blade with his hand, under the pillow. He entered her again and got up on his forearm and went inside gently. "The pain's is gone now Josh, I can only feel you." Josh was being as gentle as he could now.

He took a few big breaths and then reached for the blade under the pillow. He lifted himself up to his knees. He looked down on her and she was panting with her eyes closed. She was whispering "more Joshua, more," under her breath. He grabbed the blade from under the pillow and slit her throat as quickly as he could.

She had such a look of surprise and horror on her face. He collapsed on top of her. He looked in her eyes. She was staring at him and gurgling from the blood. He reached in and spoke in her ear. "I love you so much, they would have never let us be together," he said. "We're too beautiful to be here." "This world is not for much longer," He stared in her eyes and said, "I will see you very soon on the other side my love." "We will be together in eternity soon." "It will be wonderful, we will be together forever," Josh said as she shook, gasped for air, and bleeding all over him.

Chapter 50

ALL OF THE sudden he blacked out. When he came to, he was having an out of body experience and was floating above Jade and himself. Except it wasn't him, it was his body, but his head was bald and he had pointed Vulcan ears. All of the sudden his head turned one hundred eighty degrees and was looking up at him.

The face was like the face out of nineteen twenties vampire movie. He had red eyes and razor sharp teeth, and was looking up at him with a smile. The figure slowly looked back down at Jade, then looked back up at Josh with a laugh and then cut into Jade's her with the scalpel. He reached quickly in and Josh could hear the ribs breaking, he pulled her heart out and it was still beating.

He lunged into it and started feeding off of is like it was a big apple. He looked up at Josh again. "Tasty," it said. Josh looked down in horror. "You motherfucker," he shouted and it laughed at him.

He was back in his body again. He had blood dripping from his mouth and what was left of Jade's heart in his hand. He looked up and cried out, "GOD HOW DID I GET TO THIS PLACE." Josh was back in his body. Jade was still now, all of the life had been sucked out of her body. He looked down crying and made the incision in her belly. He reached into the gushiness of her end trails and pulled out the fetis. It had the body of a child but a piglet's head.

The piglet was staring at Josh and squealing, it was horrid. He threw the pig baby down on the bed beside Jade, and then sawed it's head off with the scalpel. He got up and put the head in his pocket and ran out the door and down the hall. The bitch clerk was standing by the office, waiting for him to come down the hall. He started running towards her.

She started taking pictures with her cell. Josh speed up and threw himself into her. She went flying one way and the cell went the other way. He got up and ran out the door. The vagrant was outside and when he saw Josh started running away from him down one of the alleyways. Josh got to the car panting, got in and got the fuck out of there.

Chapter 51

JOSH PULLED INTO his driveway and almost went through the garage door. He just wanted to get clean, get the blood off of him and get the taste Jade's heart out of his mouth. His mind was not well, not well at all. He was seeing flashbacks of Jade and the blood, so much blood. He rushed up to the door entered his code and went right for the laundry room.

He threw his clothes off and then ran upstairs to the bath room, ran the water extra hot and jumped into the shower. He held his mouth up and got the full force of the spray in his mouth, and keep it open letting the water spray in and run down his body. The taste dissipated a bit but was still there. He began scrubbing himself obsessively.

He let out a huge bellowing sigh, and grabbed himself and started rocking back and forth, shaking and sobbing horribly. He thought about Jade again and all the blood, so much blood. He started scrubbing himself again. He went over himself three times and washed his hair twice. He deemed himself clean and left the shower defeated by emotion.

He went over to the sink and grabbed the counter. His head was down and he slowly lifted it to look at himself in the mirror. He could see straight again and was in shock. Josh had always looked good for twenty seven, he often got carded for cigarettes and liquor, but now he looked like he aged so much, he looked at least thirty five. And he felt that those eight years had drained from his body as well.

Even though he had just gotten out of the shower, he splashed water in his face to compose himself. He looked again at himself and felt great sadness and guilt. He walked over to the bedroom and got dressed, he grabbed a joint off his dresser and headed down stairs. He went right for the bottle of muscovite and poured himself a half and half greyhound, and took it down quickly. He grimaced, shook his head, and he started to pour another one.

He had to get the rest of the taste of the heart out. He normally never smoked in the house but he lit a cigarette and started pacing back and fourth in his kitchen. Reality was very much starting to set in again. Josh walked out onto the patio put his cigarette out and lit the joint.

He was still pacing on the patio, went over to the ledge and yelled out, "Jade, my sweet jade," and turned and started crying again. He was taking long hauls off the joint trying to calm down. After a couple of minutes of weeping he looked up and saw Belial at the front of the patio, and man was up in the tree. He had an absolutely exhausted expression on his face and walked over to the railing to hold himself up.

Man started from the tree, "look at the state of you Josh, you're so weak, your disgusting, you actually disgust me," he said with a superior look. "Really Josh, pull yourself together man," Belial said. Josh felt rage like never before grow inside of him. He looked over at them and said "I just ate my girlfriend's fucking heart, forgive me if I'm a little rattled you fuck heads." "And you killed the pig baby Josh, Azazel will be none too impressed," man said laughing. "I got it's little fucking piglet head upstairs, do you want me to get it for you," Josh said angrily. "No, fuck the head Josh," they said both laughing, "but don't you feel better now, since the spell is gone you are now free from her."

"I am not free," Josh said with fire in his eyes, "now I feel as though she is consuming me with her revenge." "She will come and haunt me now, she will do me in just like I did her."

"You don't have to worry about that Josh, she's down with us now, in the hellfire with her constant wails of pain and pure torture." "Listen Josh can you hear her, I can, it sounds beautiful." "Fuck your mother, you fucking cocksuckers," Josh said spewing his hatred for them. "No thanks Josh," Belial said. "But we are finished with you now, the contract is null and void."

"You're going down Josh," Belial said with a smile. "We got those pictures of you to the media that the clerk took before you bowled her over." "And that's not the best part, you're going down for your company too … Yeah," Belial said laughing. "We have to have someone take the fall for it." "All the accusations that were made by that Church Josh, well they were true."

"With the illegal shipments that the company has made josh, those dead endangered species, all the humans you imported in to make human trafficking possible, and the multiple tons of coke and heroin that were smuggled into the country, you're getting nailed for all that, thanks to information that was doctored by us." "The feds seized your computer, and they did have your phone tapped all along and with your cellphone records." "They have an open and shut case." "With that, and the murder, you'll never see the light of day again."

"And when you die and your body lies stinking in the ground, remembered your God has turn his back on you for eternity." "The Nazarene has no tolerance for the taking his flock, even if their souls were corrupt." "No Josh, your fate lies with us." "And you will suffer Josh, you will be in imaginable pain and torment for all eternity, I'll make sure of it," Belial said in a monotone voice and stared Josh in the eyes."

"I'll come and piss on you while you burn Josh, just for fun," Man said. "And Jade will be beside you Josh, and I'll pull her out by her bitch hair and she'll be the house entertainment for the night." Josh just stood there stunned with his mouth open staring at them for a minute. "But I have done everything you asked," he screamed.

"Belial, I thought we were on some sort of level of understanding. "What about our talks, how can you fuck my ass like this." "Just meaningless drivel sir," and realize who you're dealing with Josh." "What did you expect … we're fucking Demons." "Filth comes out of our mouths and emanates from us."

"What I told you about the fate of humanity Josh, all that will come true." "Everything else I said was shit pouring out of my mouth." "Me too Josh," man said, "we pulled your strings like a puppet sir," "your very trainable, you should be proud of that." "But when it all came down to it Josh, Legion just did not trust you at all with your thoughts and mannerisms." "You're rebellious and you still have ties to the Nazarene within you."

The door to the patio was open and the TV turned on by itself to the news with coverage pinning him for the murder and the dealings of the company.

"That's breaking news Josh, so you still have about a ten minute start on the Feds, but there on their way now," Belial said, and turned and walked between the houses towards the street. "So go run Josh, for all it's worth, like the little rat that you are, but just remember that you belong to us my boy." "There is no hope for your life." "It's all pre destined," Man said licking his lips. Man winked again at him, gave a little push off the branch and fell into revene.

Chapter 52

JOSH TURNED AND ran into the house. He saw the remote and grabbed it. He looked up and saw his picture on the screen. He ran up to the bedroom and started thinking what was absolutely essential to bring with him. Josh was a smart boy and had been keeping some of his money in a safe at home. He didn't trust the banks for shit.

He opened it and took the thirty grand that was in there and threw it in his gym bag. He went over and got the few joints and 2 ounces of the California's finest he had left and grabbed his Giant's ball cap and Ray Ban's. He ran to the fridge downstairs held it open with his bag and threw in about 7 Strongbow tall cans he had and ran for the car leaving in the front door wide open. His neighbors across the street were looking at him stunned as jumped through the tee bar roof. He put the firebird in a quick reverse, then squealed away down the hill.

Chapter 53

JOSH HAD NO Idea where he was going and he had to think fast. Then he thought of Sergei and that he probably was the only person he could trust right now. He had a big cellar down in his bar I'm sure he could stay down there for a few days we'll things cooled down and the feds thought he fled the state. He started towards the bar. But he was going to have to ditch his car well before the bar so that he didn't have to park anywhere near it, and go the rest of the way on foot.

He got his cell phone out and was just about to press Sergei's number on speed dial but then the phone rang. He looked down but did not recognize the number. "Hello," he answered abrupt and annoyed. "Joshua," the man asked. "Yes," Josh answered. "Joshua you don't know me, my name is Michael." "What's up Michael, I'm a little preoccupied at the moment," he said annoyed. "Josh you have to listen to me and trust me blindly, it is the only way you will survive the next hour." "You can't go to Sergei's." "You have to get on the highway heading east out of San Fran." Josh look at all the things that have happened the past few months, and realized this phone call wasn't strange at all.
"

"But what if you're a demon telling lies to get me caught." "That's where that blind faith has to come into play," Michael responded. Josh new his plan wouldn't get him far enough away, and decided to trust Michael for the time being. He started towards the freeway. "Where do I go when I'm going west." "Don't fucking worry about that now," Michael said distressed, "I just got word Josh, it's going to happen in less than a half an hour." "What the fuck are you talking about," Josh said.

"How far from the freeway are you," Michael asked. "About fifteen minutes." "Get there in ten." "When you get on the highway just keep driving straight Joshua, like a bat out of hell, do you understand me," Michael shouted into the phone. Josh pulled away from the phone and calmly said, "yes." "Good," Michael replied. "Listen Josh I really got to go, there's a ton of people I got to get a hold of in the next little bit." "I'll try and get back to you within the hour, just do what I told you to do," then Michael hung up.

Josh was stopped at a light. Three blocks away was forty forth street that would take him to get onto interstate eighty. That went northeast all the way to New York. He couldn't do directly east, so this was would have to do. He got two more blocks and got stopped again by the light. He saw no cars coming so he blew the light and now he was free to get to the on ramp. He got on and started heading northeast.

ZACHARIAH LEHMANN

Chapter 54

OTIS WAS ON the radio singing about San Fran and sitting on a dock by the bay, then Otis faded and Michael voice came through the stereo. "Go Josh, faster." Josh had the firebird in fourth, and had plenty left. He was doing about ninety eight mph right then, and was weaving through the traffic. It was about one forty in the afternoon so thank God the traffic was a little lighter. "Go Josh, go faster," the voice repeated through static. Josh had a bit of a clear, straight stretch so he dropped the hammer and threw her into fifth. He saw the traffic coming up ahead. He could see a path through and his foot was on the floor.

He came up to them and the firebird started rumbling lightly, but it wasn't from the engine, it was definitely coming from the ground. It was weird but it was coming from the highway. He slowed a little and came up behind the first car. "Push harder Josh, get the fuck out like a bat out of the hell," Michael's voice shouted through the static on the radio.

He just had passed a crowded overpass and a cop motorcycle had pulled out from under it. "Don't worry about that Josh," Michael came through again, "hurry … hard!!!" Josh had her floored and started weaving in and out of the cars like a NAS car driver. Then had a straightaway for a bit so he looked in the rear view.

The firebird was now at one hundred thirty two mph and she was shrieking at him, she couldn't put out any more. He looked in his rearview mirror He could still see the bay and downtown through an intense brown cloud but it was not smog covering it, it was way thicker and coming from the ground. And then Josh saw, even though faintly, that the downtown had slightly angled itself towards the ocean. The firebird was really shaking now and the car had started jumping slightly from the tremors beneath it. All the traffic ahead of him had pulled over to the side, the people were out and just staring back at the city.

He looked back, the cop was gone and the overpass that he had passed about forty seconds ago that was packed with cars, seemed to crack and just fall apart, causing a crackling noise. The shaking from the road hit its peak and then started to die quickly. Josh refused to look back, he was just looking forward with terror in his eyes. The Firebird just hit one thirty eight.

ZACHARIAH LEHMANN

Chapter 55

JOSH GOT TO Sacramento just after ten pm. Everyone seemed very distant and Josh didn't even ask about what had happened in San Francisco. He still had heard anything more from Michael. Josh was really scared, he had placed all his faith and his future in this man he didn't know. But it looked like he had helped him get of a really bad spot at home. And he heard in Michael's voice that he was sincere in what he was saying. Josh got back in the car, cracked a can and kept going. He started thinking of Jade and the helpless look on her face as she bleed out.

He was crying again and was swearing to avenge her. About another half hour down the road, Josh got a call. "Hello, Michael," Josh said anxiously. "Yes Josh, I'm here." "What happened back home." "I'll be seeing you very soon and we'll have a little chat." "We're am I meeting you?" "Carson City," Michael replied. "When you get into town, get off at exit ninety six and follow the road to the right". "Follow that road for about 5 minutes and you'll see an all night diner on the left." "It's called Annie's." "I'll meet you there in about oh, Michael paused, around one." "Got it," Josh said, "see you soon," and Michael was gone.

Chapter 56

H E PULLED INTO the dinner about twelve forty. Josh finished his Strongbow and threw it on the back floor of the car. He got out and made his way into the diner. He got in and surveyed the place. There was young beautiful Native American waitress, who gave him a big welcoming smile. There were two Greek guys eating breakfast and having a heated argument at the table in front of him.

He looked to the left and there was a guy with platinum blonde hair by the window drinking his coffee and reading the paper. He looked over to the booth and there was a huge burly biker looking guy, just staring at him with his bandana and sunglasses on.

"Hey Josh, why don't you come and have a seat," he said. Josh went over to the table and Josh stuck out his hand and said "Michael?" Michael shook his hand and said "the one and only." Josh sat down and the waitress came over and dropped off a menu. "Coffee," she said. "No, I never touch the stuff, could you bring me a Bud," Josh said giving the menu back. "Sure hunny, I'll be right back," she said.

Josh looked back over at Michael, "so who are you and how do I know you," Josh started. "Better question is how doyou know me, and why did you save me." "What happened back there in California, did you know Jade," Josh continued. "Slow down Josh," "we have lots of time to talk," he said calmly. Michael took his glasses off and the waitress came over and gave him his beer with another big smile.

"Well, I guess I'll start with California." "The big one hit Josh, pretty much half of the west coast states are in the water right now." "News reports have been scattered and unclear, so the rest of the country doesn't really know the full immensity of the destruction yet." "Needless to say, no one is going to be looking for you for what you've done."

"I've known you in heaven since before you were born to this earth Joshua, when you were in the hall of souls." "I know you better than anyone does except for Christ himself." "I did know Jade, and I have been following both of you since you met." "I'm sorry for you loss, I know how you felt about her." And it wasn't just the spell, do you love her any less now." You two were coerced by evil Josh, you two were vulnerable, and Legion took advantage of that." "They had you do a lot of evil in their name Josh."

"Josh they don't have your soul." "What," Josh said. "It was never yours to sell." "Your soul belongs to Christ and Jade." "Who are you," Josh questioned. "Well Josh, I'm the arch Angel Michael." "No shit," Josh said amazed.

"What Belial told you was true, you are marked for salvation." "What he didn't know was that Satan cannot possess the soul of a person who is marked." "That's such a good thing, I feel so much better," Josh said, "that takes so much weight off my shoulders." Josh said. "And what you said to Jade when she was dying, about that you would be together in another world and that you would see her soon, you were talking the truth." "She's at peace Josh and waiting for you on the other side." Josh started weeping in happiness. "The Rapture is coming very soon." "I'm talking full book of Revelation shit," Michael continued. "And Joshua I need your help to get us prepared."

"The antichrist is already on earth, he's been here for twenty seven years now, you two actually share the same birthday." "Within the next three months, world religions will be obsolete, people will basically putting their allegiance in either good or evil." "And evil will heavily out way the good." "But that doesn't necessarily mean that they have the advantage." "It's the whole quality verses quantity thing." "We're quality Josh."

Chapter 57

"THERE WAS ANOTHER thing Belial said to you that was true." "God is dead Josh." Josh just looked at him with his mouth wide open. "I guess in human terms you could say he committed suicide." "He couldn't take the path man had chosen and that the world had become inherently evil." "God became void Josh." "He became one of the biggest black holes in the universe." "There has been no contact with him since." "We don't know if it's possible that he comes back from where he is, which is nothingness."

"But Christ and the Holy Ghost are very much alive." "Jesus has undying faith in humanity after he died for you people." "They will be leading us in battle and will do a lot of damage in the War to end all Wars." Josh was just listen and trying to take it all in.

"The white haired man that was sitting by the window, stood up and started making his way over to the table." He sat down beside Michael and was just clocking Josh. He finally said, "You're a real piece of shit, you know."

"Your mind is so weak that you let the darkness into your life." "And those men you killed, they were repenting and helping other people survive in their lives." "And you know the three marks on your shoulder Belial gave to you, that's like spitting in Michael and my face." "It's the mocking of the trinity." "I know," Josh said ashamed." "I think you should get up and leave." "I think you should go and find a hole in the ground and hide in it until the war is over, you're useless and weak." "Go now, the man shouted at him."

Josh just sat there with his head down. Michael was not sticking up for him. He then raised his head and said "Im a good person I know that, and I'm not going anywhere." "Good for you Josh, don't take no shit from him," Michael said. "Josh I want you to meet Gabriel." Gabriel and Josh then both started smiling and they shook hands over the table.

"I was just trying to see if you were easily influenced Josh, you did well," Gabriel said. Gabriel almost looked exactly like Belial, except that he had blonde hair and green eyes." "Yeah we were brothers before the fall," Gabriel said reading Josh's thoughts.

"So Josh," Michael continued, "we are gathering those that are marked and those with them that have taken our side." "I have a serious duty for you." "Consider this repentance for what you have done to help the dark one."

Chapter 58

"THERE IS A tribe in the Brazilian Amazon called the Kayapo." "They are all marked for salvation, and we need them, they will be some of our fiercest warriors for us in battle." "In this tribe's folklore, it tells of a white man that will come and lead them to the great battle." "How will they know I'm the one," Josh asked. "Well first of all you'll be the first white man they have seen in a very long time, and also you will bring them this symbol," Michael said and handed Josh the symbol.

"It will tell them that the prophecy has come true, and they will follow you out without question." "But the odds are definitely against you." "First of all, there's the other tribes in there, you'll have to pass through their territory and they'd love to have a white man's head on a stick for one of their ceremonies." "Then there's the disease Josh, the immunizations don't always work." "But we have a guide who's going to take you in there."

"He speaks English and was a part of the Kawahiva tribe in there up until he left about ten years ago." "He knows the area and the other tribe's territories well, and he knows of the Kayapo and where to find them." "What about the snakes and the spiders and all the other shit that can kill you in there." "You'll do most of your travelling by boat on the river, and the guide knows how to set up camp in there so you're pretty safe where that's concerned," Gabriel said.

"And Joshua, there is also the very real possibility that the dark one will be following you in there, trying to whatever it takes for you to fail." "And he'll fuck with your mind Josh and everything you believe, you must be mentally and spiritually ready for what he throws at you." "It won't be Belial this time, It will be Lucifer himself."

"Why doesn't the guide just go in and get them," Josh said. "The Kayapo has to see the symbol from a white man Josh, remember I told you," Michael said. "Josh you can't refuse this." "You need to do this as repentance for your earthly sins and to become pure again." Josh was just sitting in the both rocking back and forth. "What do you think Lucifer will try to do to me," Josh asked. "He might not even be in there with you, but if he is just realize not everything is as what it seems," Gabriel continued.

"I don't know what he might do to you, but he will come to you at your weakest point, when you have given up faith and when you have too much fear to go on." "Be strong Joshua," Gabriel said. "He'll feed on fear and weaknesses." "You'll have to overcome this Josh, this is not something we can help you with."

"You have to face this or you'll be lost Josh." "What do you mean lost," Josh asked. "You will be useless to us, your soul will wonder forever in torture," Gabriel said. "There is no choice then is there," Josh said. "No, there really isn't," Michael replied. "And if you survive this quest, you will come back to us a great warrior for the cause."

"Once you get out them out, your guide will take you and them into French Guiana where there will be a ship waiting for you in the port of Cayenne." "From there, the ship will take you and the tribe to Halifax, Nova Scotia." "I will meet you there," Michael said. "I have a friend that's sympathetic to our cause in Canadian customs that will get them in as Syrian refugees." "The Canadians will take care of them until there needed." "Josh got the menu back and ordered a steak sandwich and the three of them talked for a bit."

"So Josh," Michael started, "you're going to drive New York and then pick up your ticket at the United counter at JFK." "You have two days to get there so don't dilly dally." "Here, Michael handed him a closed envelope. "This is all the info you need for when you get to Brazil, you know how to find the guide and where to stay, your bank account info and so on."

"Josh you should get some sleep before you start driving." "We booked a room for you at the Best Western down the road," Gabriel said. As they stood up, Michael looked down on him. "Josh this is the single most important thing you will do in your life, for yourself and for our side."

"We both have faith in you," Gabriel was nodding, "and we know that you can do this." "I'll be in touch before you get into the jungle, but after that you'll be on your own with the guide." "God speed my friend," and they both gave him a hug and they left. Joshua left and made his way to the hotel. He got upstairs and he didn't want a drink, he was too tired. He sat down in bed and though, this is going to be a long couple of months. When he finally slept he was tortured by night terrors of the ghosts of the past, and the evil that will confront him in the near future. He begged to Christ to give him the strength and resolve to succeed in his mission.

The world was about to change in a very ominous way. Josh knew he would be a major player in the new order that soon would be established. He was so afraid of the unknown, but he couldn't do anything about it. He just hope he ended up on the winning side of the war that was about to come.

Printed in the United States
By Bookmasters